MISTLETOE NOT REQUIRED

A. D. JUSTICE

A.D. Justice

MISTLETOE NOT REQUIRED.

This is my first trip home in nearly four years. I haven't been back for a very good reason—and his name is Hunter Beckett.

My parents need my help over Christmas break, so I've agreed to return during the semester break against my better judgment.

Kisses under the mistletoe. Family pictures in front of the numerous decorations. Christmas in Cringle Cove is a magical time for everyone else who visits —just not for me.

Four long years away without a single glance backward. I'm THISCLOSE to college graduation. One week around the chocolate-with-flecks-of-gold-eyed devil and I'm THISCLOSE to giving in to him all over again.

Hunter should come with a warning label: MISTLETOE NOT REQUIRED.

CHAPTER ONE

Mallory

"I hate this town. When we left for college, I swore I'd never come back here. I almost made it to graduation without a single return visit—until now." My stomach churns and my heart races as I automatically scan the crowds, looking for *him*—Hunter Beckett. How I can simultaneously want to see him and not want to see him is still a mystery. But there it is anyway.

"Mallory, how can you hate this place? It's awesome! I can't believe I've never been here before. I also can't believe you've kept this from me for all these years we've lived together." Amelia, my best friend and partner in crime, is originally from Georgia and made the long drive back home with me so I wouldn't be alone. Her head looks as if it's on a swivel, trying to catch a glimpse of every Christmas-decorated storefront in town. Which, by the way, is every single one of them.

As I drive down Main Street in the small town in northeastern Pennsylvania where I grew up, I quickly realize nothing has changed in the last few years since I left. Winter always brings the tourists into our quaint little village. Strings of bright white lights are wound around every tree trunk and bare limb and also dutifully line every store eave. Professionally decorated wreaths hang from every lamppost illuminating the sidewalks of Main Street.

Even I have to admit the elaborate trimmings set against the snowcapped mountains create the perfect illusion of being at the North Pole with Santa. But I'll never admit that out loud.

"The city council members know the livelihoods of most of the business owners depend on the influx of tourists, especially during the week of Christmas. Every business goes all out to make this place even better than Santa's workshop itself."

"Well, it's working. I already want to move here and stay forever."

"Be careful what you wish for, Amelia—you may just get it. That wouldn't be a good thing in this case. I'm afraid of being sucked back into the black hole of Cringle Cove and being stuck here forever myself."

The idyllic mountain setting, complete with a virtually guaranteed white Christmas, brings families from near and far. Rooms in the local hotels and bed-and-breakfast inns are booked solid several months in advance by families looking for a little slice of Christmas heaven. And in the days leading up to the holiday, the intense draw to spend a holiday vacation here is obvious. Everyone in this town feels like a little kid on Christmas morning again for a few days, but reality lurks in the shadows, never too far away.

Reality bites.

"Is that snow? Oh my gosh, Mallory—it's snowing!"

"It's just a few flurries, Amelia. Don't get too excited. It's not like we're in a blizzard or anything."

Snow is a rare occasion at the University of Georgia where we attend together. Snow at Christmas is almost unheard of down south, where I can almost wear shorts right up until the January cold spell hits…and lasts for about thirteen days before the temperature begins to rise again. No such luck in my hometown. It is cold all winter long. And it snows—a lot.

As if the weather isn't enough reason to avoid Cringle Cove, that jackass Hunter Beckett still lives here. I want to run into him almost as much as I want to run head first and butt naked into a snowdrift.

All excellent reasons for staying away. Permanently.

"Conner Veterinary Services—there's your parents' business. It's so cool they're both veterinarians." Amelia bounces in her seat while she points toward the sign hanging prominently over the front door. I can't help but laugh at her enthusiasm. This is a two-red-light town, so it's a little hard to miss anything.

"Yep, that's it—and it's all decked out for the holidays. I always loved working in their office when I was a kid. I learned so much from just watching them treat the animals."

"I'm so excited about helping your dad while your mom helps your grandmother."

"Me too. I'm just glad we didn't draw the short straw like Mom did."

After I park in front of the building, Amelia and I step out of the car and immediately tighten our coats against the icy December wind. We make a beeline out of the cold into the clinic to find my dad. The interior of the building is both familiar and surreal. Everything looks the same, but it feels like much longer than the almost four years since I last stepped foot in here. The same old bell is mounted over the doorframe, jingling a soft tune every time the door opens. The receptionist desk is still front and center, waiting to greet the patients and their owners. The door to the exam rooms in the back of the building is still to the left of the desk. The old wood floors still creak in certain spots but also give the clinic a more home-like feel.

Trusting my senses is becoming more and more difficult, and I've only been back for a few minutes. That's because of the black hole syndrome—the intense gravity draws me in before suffocating me in total darkness.

I haven't seen my dad in way too long, and a pang of guilt hits me like a sledgehammer to the chest. I grew up in this office with my parents, working side by side with them even before I was old enough to actually help. Nostalgia hits me unexpectedly, and I instantly feel like I'm home again. The entire time I've been away at college, I've chanted over and over about how much I hate it here and how I never wanted to return. Give me two minutes inside the city limits, and I'm right back to being a little kid again.

"Mallory! Come give your old man a hug." Dad walks through the doorway from the direction of exam rooms and extends his arms out to each side, wide open for me to rush into them, and I do without missing a beat. He wraps his strong arms around me and squeezes tightly.

"Hi, Daddy. I've missed you." I slide my arms around his neck and pull closer to him.

"I've missed you too, sweetheart. It's so good to have you home again."

Before I start crying like a little schoolgirl, I release him and take a step back. "Daddy, you remember Amelia."

"Of course. She's the second daughter we never had. Where's my hug, Amelia?"

Like a moth to a flame, she flies into Daddy's arms without waiting for a second request. After Amelia's father passed away when she was a baby, her mom never remarried. Over the past several years, my parents have visited us in Georgia, and my dad has made it his mission to help fill that hole in Amelia's life.

"Thank you so much for letting me crash your family's Christmas, Pete. I would've been all alone if I'd stayed home. Mom and her friends are off on a girls' skiing trip."

"It's not crashing when you're part of the family, honey. We've already claimed you as one of our own. Hang up your coats on the rack over there, then I'll show you around the office before we meet Jackie for dinner."

"Mom's not sitting with Gran?" Like a little kid, I cross my fingers behind my back, hoping Dad won't say Gran is joining us too.

"She was, but we hired a sitter to help with *my* mom so *your* mom can spend some time with you since you're home for the first time in forever." His left eyebrow lifts slightly and his gaze remains locked on mine, leaving no doubt he knows I have no interest in seeing Gran today. Or any other day of the year, for that matter.

While Dad shows Amelia around the office, my mind drifts back to the days and weeks when I worked here with him. All the supplies are kept in the same places they've always been. I only half listen as Dad explains the procedures for taking care of the crated animals—I remember exactly how to care for them. An older black-and-white dog catches my attention, so I stop at his crate and check on him. Amelia, on the other hand, hangs on Dad's every word, soaking up the instructions and trying to memorize what is kept where, and she doesn't even notice I'm no longer following them around.

She's naturally an overachiever.

The bell over the front door rings, but I barely notice it since the dog I'm petting apparently likes me as much as I like him.

"Hey, Dr. Conner. How's it going? Is Banjo ready to come home yet?"

That voice…I'd know that voice anywhere. Panic steals my breath, and my lungs seize in my chest. My hand remains on the sweet dog, keeping him from exiting the crate, but I can't move.

Hunter Beckett is here.

In this very building.

And he's picking up an animal.

Survival instincts kick in, and I snap out of my daze. With a quick kiss to his forehead, I whisper an apology to my new friend for leaving him so abruptly before I swiftly close the crate door.

"Hey, Hunter. How are you? He's ready and waiting for you. Give me a minute to show Amelia how to get him out of the crate, then we'll bring him up here." Dad's voice echoes in the hall, growing closer to me as he speaks.

"Take your time, Doc. I'm not in a hurry."

The door to the boarding area starts to open, and my fight-or-flight senses kick in. I bolt through the door leading to the fenced area outside—right into the cold wind and spitting snow. Without my coat.

This was a really stupid move. What was I thinking? Hunter wasn't joining us in the back, and I would've been completely blocked from his view had I moved one foot to the left or the right. Instead, I lost control of myself just because I heard his stupid, sexy, manly voice. Mentally psyching myself up, I draw my shoulders back and hold my head up high.

"I'm going back in there. This is ridiculous."

I reach for the cold brass doorknob and give it a good, swift turn, ready to stroll back in and face the music like an adult. Except...the door automatically locked behind me, effectively thwarting my plan.

"Oh God. No, no, no, no." I try the door again, but it seems at least one thing works right this evening—the door lock is doing its job.

A gust of arctic wind blasts through my clothes, and it feels like I'm not even wearing anything, automatically forcing me to circle my arms around my body in a tight hug and a desperate attempt for warmth. Of course, that doesn't help at all since the wind just continues to slice through me. With my face down and my whole body shivering, I work my way over to the chain link fence and rush around to the front of the building.

"What the..." A search of my pockets comes up empty —no keys to even hide out in the car until Hunter leaves. "Just my freaking luck. Seriously."

Unable to hold out any longer, I trudge to the door and rush inside.

"Uh...Mallory?" Amelia's surprised and alarmed tone barely hides the hint of humor underneath. The problem is, my mind is still frozen from the cold, but my body is very much aware of the electricity Hunter naturally exudes. Bad thing is, electricity can be deadly. Especially in this case.

"Yeah?" I refuse to make eye contact in my attempt to play it cool. Or cold. Whatever.

"Why were you outside...in the cold...without your coat...or a hat?"

"It's not that bad. I walked around from the back, just looking around. It has been a long time since I was here."

"I'd say it has been almost four years since she was last home. Isn't that right, Pete?"

My eyes betray me at the sound of Hunter's voice, and they rise with a slow perusal, taking in his form from his work boot-covered feet to the top of his head. He's taller than when I left—and definitely more muscular. The handsome boy I knew grew into a fine, *fine* man. He filled out in all the right places. His hair is cut short but still almost the same shade of brown as mine. Those eyes, though—the swirls of chocolate brown and golden flecks—still make me weak in the knees. Then one side of his mouth lifts slightly in amusement—a dead giveaway he knows I'm checking him out.

Bastard.

"You're right, Hunter. And I've missed my little girl every day during all those years."

"I'm only back for a couple of weeks over our semester break to help Dad while Mom sits with Gran."

Hunter's smile slowly fades at the mention of Gran, as I knew it would. She has a way of putting a damper on anything. "Welcome home. I'm sure your family is glad you're home, even if it's only for a short time."

"Actually, home is in Georgia now. This is just a short visit." I'm trying to convince myself as much as anyone else.

"Semantics. You say visit, I say homecoming. Same thing. Anyway, I'd better get Banjo home and let you three finish up here, then. Thanks again, Doc."

"You bet, Hunter. Don't be a stranger."

He walks toward the door, giving Dad a single nod in response. The ultimate noncommittal response. Something he was all too familiar with when I knew him as a teenager, and apparently, he hasn't changed since then. Other than his bigger muscles. And the way he fills out his worn jeans. And that overtly masculine five o'clock shadow that I want to scrape my fingernails across.

"Mallory." Amelia sounds like a frustrated mother when she says my name before grabbing my shoulders, pulling me out of my Hunter-induced haze. She twirls me to face her and begins running her fingers through my hair, smoothing it down in places and completely rearranging it in others. "You look like you were caught in a tornado and it intentionally turned your hair into a bird's nest. You want to tell me what you were really doing outside now that he's gone?"

I groan loudly and rush to the mirror hanging in the waiting area. "Oh. My. Freaking. God!" Amelia's fingers soon join mine in a mad dash to tame the wild beast that has taken over my head. This day just keeps getting better and better.

Dad chuckles to himself when he walks away, checking the doors and turning off the lights before we leave to meet Mom.

"You don't have to worry about checking the back door, Daddy. It locks just fine."

His laughter echoes through the empty building as he walks through the door to the back, making me smile in spite of myself.

"You're going to explain what happened here. You know I don't like being left out in the cold like this." Amelia leans toward me, poking me with her finger for added emphasis.

"Don't even talk to me about being left out in the cold

right now. I still haven't thawed out after my trip around the block."

"Ready to go meet your mother?" Dad picks up our coats and helps each of us into them. "She can't wait to see her girls."

CHAPTER TWO

Hunter

Even with her windblown hair and crazy lie about walking around the block without a coat, Mallory Conner is still the most beautiful woman I've ever seen. It has been far too many years since I've seen her live and in color, and she sounds determined to continue her disappearing act as soon as her Christmas break ends.

I'm equally as determined to make sure that doesn't happen. By any means necessary.

"Let's get you inside, buddy."

With a sixty-five-pound dog in my arms, I hurry into the house and deposit him onto his bed. The dog gets more attention than I do, that's for sure.

"Mom, Dad, where are you two? I brought Banjo home for you."

Mom joins me in the living room and goes straight to Banjo. "Thank you, Hunter. Your dad is in his man cave, hanging upside down on the inversion table. His back still hurts, and he refuses to go to the doctor. There's no way he could've carried Banjo all the way from the car. I'm so glad you were around to bring him back home. I've missed my buddy."

"He was only gone for one night, Mom. He just got neutered—it's not a big deal. He didn't even realize you weren't around."

"Of course he did. I bet he was glad to see you at the vet's office, wasn't he?"

"He was," I admit. *Too bad he was the only one glad to see me.* "I'm heading out now. I'll see you later."

After a quick kiss to my mom's cheek, I rush back to my truck and head right back into town. On my way to my parents' farm, I noticed a few familiar faces in the picture window of the best restaurant in town, Diner on Main. Max Kenrick and Shaine Prescott were walking out, looking a little cozier than last time I saw them. Camry and Tessa, a couple of sisters from the area I've known forever, were there too. And Jackie, Mallory's mother, was also there. She was sitting alone at a table for four, so Mallory, Amelia, and Pete must be joining her soon. One more place setting at that large table shouldn't be a problem. The window of opportunity to win Mallory back won't stay open for long, especially when she's made it clear she intends to slam it shut as soon as her break is over. This is a now-or-never situation. Good thing there's no time like the present.

After snagging the last available parking spot at the end of the block, I jump out of my truck and sprint toward the restaurant, zigging and zagging around the window-shopping tourists. After living here all my life, I should be used to the crowds that show up around Christmas. And I know I should be grateful to them for helping to make my business so successful. But right now, it feels like every single one of them is standing between Mallory and me.

After what feels like an eternity, but in reality has only been about sixty seconds, I'm finally inside the swanky bistro with one Mallory Conner sitting directly in my line of sight. She's busy talking to her mom, her arms and hands animatedly adding to the conversation, so she doesn't notice me approaching the table at first. The closer I get to her, the stronger I feel the pull inside my chest. The invisible connection isn't one-sided either. I know she feels it too.

She proves my theory when her mouth abruptly stops moving and her head turns toward me before I've said a single word. Time slows to a crawl as I wind through the tables and chairs separating us, undeterred from my goal. Our eyes meet from across the room, and neither of us is able to look away. That is, until a passing waitress unwittingly steps too close to Mallory's elaborate arm gestures and gets caught in the cross fire.

Mallory had stopped talking with her mouth, but her arms were still very much in motion. When we were kids, I'd always tease her by saying she'd be mute if I tied her hands behind her back. Apparently, her hand catching the waitress's tray just right and causing every plate and glass on it to crash to the floor in front of a packed restaurant also does the trick. Mallory's hands fly to her mouth, covering the gaping hole in her face. Her eyes are wide open, unblinking and unmoving from the mounds of wasted food and drinks.

Even with pure humiliation creeping up her neck and covering her face, making Rudolph's nose pale in comparison, she still completely captivates me. The smile spreading across my face has nothing to do with the disastrous scene set squarely between us and everything to do with this fiasco fitting exactly how I remember Mallory. Well-meaning but a walking disaster. Somehow equally graceful and clumsy. How she pulled off that combination always amazed me, and I'm glad to see some things never change.

Mallory grabs the linen napkin from her lap and flies out of her seat, facing the soaked waitress, Tasha, according to her name tag. I can read Mal's every thought like an open book from the emotions crossing her face.

She starts to reach out with the napkin to dry Tasha's shirt.

But where do I start?

She tentatively extends her hand then quickly withdraws it.

I probably shouldn't touch her there.

She puts the napkin down on the table before her knees slightly bend.

I can't use my hands to clean up that mess.

The thing is, I can hear her saying all of this like she's in my head. The truth is, she's been in my head for many years now.

"What can I do?" She finally just asks Tasha for direction.

"You don't have to do anything, ma'am. It's okay—I have another shirt in the back. It'll only take me a minute to go change."

Without even realizing I'm doing it, I shift my weight to one leg, cross my arms over my chest, and watch her with rapt attention, a smile permanently etched on my face. My Mallory is back in town, and it's way past time for the two of us to get up close and personal again.

The manager rushes over and reassures Mallory he will take care of everything. After he convinces her to take her seat, several busboys work together to clean up the mess until no trace of it is left. The other patrons lost interest immediately after the initial collision, resuming their conversations so a dull roar carries through the room. Everything returns to normal, with customers coming and going, yet Mallory still hides her face behind her napkin. When she finally lowers it back to her lap, I know the very second she remembers I'm standing nearby. Our eyes lock again, and fury replaces her embarrassment.

That is the moment when I realize I'm still smiling.

"Oh shit." I mutter the words under my breath when she excuses herself from the table and stomps toward me.

"What's so funny, Hunter?" The fire in her eyes is meant to intimidate me, but all it does is stoke the old flame between us.

"I wasn't laughing, Mallory." The hint of laughter in my voice definitely makes me sound like a liar. In my defense, I actually didn't laugh.

"Care to explain what that shit-eating grin's all about, then?"

"Why do you sound like you've been south of the Mason-Dixon line for more than the last few years?"

"Amelia's a bad influence on me. Stop changing the subject. I asked you a question."

With a slight bend at the waist, I invade her personal space and put us at eye level. "My shit-eating grin is all about you, Mal. Always has been. Always will be. I'm glad to see you haven't changed much since you've been gone."

"That's where you're wrong, Hunter. I absolutely have changed."

"Hunter, good to see you. Have you had dinner yet?" Pete appears next to Mallory before she makes another scene.

"No, sir. I haven't."

"That's great—come join us. We haven't ordered yet, and there's plenty of room."

Mallory's head may do a three-sixty any second now if the glare she's giving her dad is any indication. But then, her spunk always was the spice of our relationship.

"Thanks, Pete. I appreciate the offer. I'd like that."

When he returns to the table to grab another chair, her gaze swings back to me and her bottom jaw drops. "What the *fuuu*—"

Leaning toward her, I whisper in her ear. "Wow, that Southern accent is more pronounced than I realized. Very sexy. You'll want to hold on to that. I'd like to hear you screaming my name in that sweet, twangy sound." The bright red sunburned look she'd only recovered from a few seconds ago is back in full force.

I step around Mallory and greet her mother with a hug and a kiss on her cheek. "Hi Jackie, how are you? You look beautiful as always."

"You're so sweet, Hunter. Thank you. I couldn't be better. I'm so happy to have my baby girl home for Christmas. How are your parents? I haven't seen them around town lately."

"Same as always. Dad threw his back out again and refuses to see the doctor. So he stays home and drives Mom crazy."

Four of the five people at the table laugh, under-standing all too well how family members can be. Everyone but Mallory. When I look across the table at her, a small smile plays on her lips, but she's trying to fight it. As if she doesn't want to remember what it's like being around her family and old friends more often.

Interesting.

After we place our orders, I catch Mallory staring at me several times while we tell Amelia stories from our past. Not our past as a couple, but our collective past as kids growing up in this winter wonderland getaway. The sly childhood antics we tried to pull that were obvious to every adult around us. The way Mallory looks at me gives me hope and pushes my agenda even more to convince her we belong together.

"You actually poured the whole bottle of bubble bath in the town fountain?" Amelia obviously hasn't heard this story from Mallory before now, judging by the shocked look on her face. "I mean, you know what happens when you put a capful in the bathtub. But you poured the whole bottle in?"

Mallory releases a heavy sigh before explaining what happened back then. "I blame the cartoons we watched. They set unreasonable expectations of what would happen. I thought it would fill the town with tiny bubbles, floating through the air and making it even more magical than it already was. Reality was much different, though. Picture an episode of *I Love Lucy* on bubble-powered steroids. Rather than the small, delicate orbs I envisioned, it was an unending wall of foam that covered the entire fountain, crawled over the edge, and across the entire lawn in front of city hall. They had to cancel the Easter egg hunt that year because of me. The more they used the water hoses to try to clear it all off, the worse it became."

"Mal, why didn't you ever tell me about any of this before? What happened to that fun, spontaneous Mallory?"

"You mean the one who was grounded and had to clean animal poop from every cage, every single day, from

Easter until the end of summer? That Mallory learned her lesson and didn't pull that stunt again."

"That's right," Jackie adds. "That Mallory didn't pull that stunt again. She pulled all new ones, like sneaking out of her window at night to go skinny-dipping in the lake with her best friend, only to be brought home by the chief of police. You know, Chief Land still warns kids against that in his own version of scared straight stories at the high school."

"Oh, thank God, the food is here. Everyone feel free to stuff your mouths and stop talking about me now."

The adventurous Mallory is still in there—I see the gleam in her eyes while she relives those memories. I'll be glad to help her find that side of her personality again... but hopefully without joining the Polar Bear Club while she's home.

"Hey Mal, remember that year when Old Man Kirkman played the town Santa Claus? Did you ever tell your parents about that?"

"Um, let me answer that. No. She didn't. Mallory, would you like to share with us now?" Pete lowers his fork to his plate, steeples his fingers together, and lifts one eyebrow at Mallory. That has been his signature move to elicit a confession for as long as I've known him.

"No, I'm good. Thanks for asking, though." Mallory stuffs an extra-large bite of her food into her mouth and chews exaggeratedly, moaning occasionally for added effect. "This is so good. You should really eat while it's hot."

"Every kid makes cookies for Santa, right? Mallory made a special batch of Oreo cookies for him. She scraped all the white filling out of them and replaced it with toothpaste, presented them to Mr. Kirkman while she sat on his lap, and waited for him to eat a couple of them before she would get down." I smile widely and work hard to hold in my laughter.

"Mallory Alexandra Conner—you did not do that to Mr. Kirkman!" Jackie looks horrified while Amelia giggles uncontrollably.

"That was just the first day." All eyes turn to me as I throw gasoline on the fire. "The second day, she climbed up on his lap and gave him an ice cream cone."

"Well, that was a nice gesture. What am I missing?" Amelia asked.

"The ice cream was actually Mom's leftover mashed potatoes," Mallory admits, and Jackie hides her face.

"It was after day three when Mr. Kirkman banned her from seeing or talking to Santa ever again."

"She was banned from Santa? What in the world did she do?" Amelia's eyes dart between Mallory and me, waiting to see who will respond first.

"Day three was a multifaceted attack. She'd planned these pranks all year. With all the tourists in town, the public restrooms stayed full, and Santa couldn't be away from his public throne very long while he used the private throne. There was only one restroom Mr. Kirkman could use—the one in the veterinary clinic, because it was the least-used by tourists."

"What did you do to that poor man?" Pete stares at the top of Mallory's head, because she has her face practically buried in her plate, actively avoiding making eye contact with anyone.

"She took a pair of your old pants and work boots and set them up like someone was in the stall. She locked the stall door and crawled out from underneath. Mr. Kirkman must've gone in and out of the clinic ten times before he was able to do his business.

"Only, when he finally got inside the stall, he didn't realize she'd covered the toilet opening with clear plastic wrap. We could hear him cursing all the way down the hall. Then, she replaced the bar of soap with one she'd covered with clear nail polish so he couldn't lather up no matter how hard he tried.

"He rambled all through the clinic, mumbling about how there had to be soap somewhere since you worked with animals all the time. He heard her giggling from her hiding place, so he yelled that she could never tell Santa what she wanted for Christmas again because he had put her name on the Naughty List."

"Wait just a minute. Let me get something straight." The expression on Amelia's face doesn't bode well for me. I can feel it in my gut. "You were there with her during all these pranks where Mallory got in trouble?"

I suddenly feel the need to plead the Fifth.

"Of course. We were best friends as kids—we did everything together."

"Well then, Hunter. It sounds to me like you were the bad influence on her."

I'm stunned speechless for a moment before my gaze moves over to Mallory.

Now who's wearing a shit-eating grin?

CHAPTER THREE

Mallory

Amelia flops down across the bed in my old room and props her chin up on her hands. The cunning smile plastered on her face is not a good sign…for me. "You've only mentioned Hunter once or twice since I met you during our freshman year. You never said anything about how sexy he is. Those brown eyes with gold flecks and his naturally muscular build. How serious were you two?"

"We were kids." I cringe when I realize I used the exact same words Gran used to describe us just under four years ago. During my senior year in high school. When he dumped me without warning and crushed my heart. "He's three years older than me, but we dated all through my high school years. He was my first."

"Any chance for a reconciliation?"

"None." My emphatic tone leaves little room for argument. I turn to rummage through my suitcase, looking for my pajamas.

"No chance of reconciling with your first love, huh? Then you won't mind if I make him my last."

I've changed my mind—there is a lot of room for argument.

My voice is a little louder than I intended when I whirl around to face her. "What the hell, Amelia? Have you lost your mind?"

A slow, satisfied smile crawls across her face. "Seems like an especially strong response for someone who has no desire to rekindle a relationship with her ex-boyfriend."

"My relationship with Hunter was a long time ago, and it was also *over* a long time ago. Regardless of how strong my reaction to your idea of marrying him and living happily ever after is, I still can't see a different outcome than the one we're in right now."

"Maybe you need to take a step back, then. Because from where I was sitting during dinner, I can plainly see that man is still in love with you."

"He's an ex for a reason, Amelia. He broke my heart. I guess, in a really sad way, I should thank him. His betrayal was a huge contributing factor in why I chose to attend UGA. And if not for that choice, I wouldn't have met you."

"You should forgive him for that reason alone. I mean, having me in your life is worth more than whatever heart-break you endured in your pre-Amelia years."

Her sarcastic wit always cheers me up. She doesn't sugarcoat anything for me, and she doesn't pat me on the head and tell me everything will be all right in the end. She does remind me of what's important, though, and expects me to put on my big-girl panties and deal with the situation head on.

"There's nothing to forgive anymore. It was a long time

ago, and I've moved on, so there's no reason to hold on to a grudge."

She laughs out loud—her sarcastic, disbelieving, I'm-calling-you-on-your-bullshit laugh. "Girl, who do you think you're talking to here? I know you better than anyone. You still have the hots for him just as much as he does for you. Moved on, my ass."

"Shut up."

"Oh, good comeback, Mal. You really burned me with that one. I may never recover from the gaping wound in my ego that response left in its wake." She rolls over onto her back and stretches out, content in her wittiness. "So, when do I get to meet this wonderful grandmother of yours?"

After several heartbeats of silence, Amelia moves to sit on the side of the bed, staring at me with her eyebrows drawn down and her head slightly cocked to the side. Silence isn't a common occurrence between the two of us.

"Hopefully never, because that would mean I'd have to be around her again."

"What'd she do to you, Mallory? What happened?"

"I overheard her telling Hunter he'd be better off without me. That we weren't a good fit, I'd ruin any plans he had for his life, and he should find someone better. The next day, he broke up with me."

"Did you talk to her about it? Surely, you misunderstood her words or why she said those things."

"No, I didn't talk to her, but I also didn't misunderstand anything. She has always been controlling and domineering. She thinks she owns everyone and can rule them with an iron fist. One of my earliest memories of her was when she tried to break up my parents' marriage. She never liked my mom when they were dating, and she liked her even less after they got married. There was a huge fight at our house—but my parents stuck together and told her to leave. They didn't speak to her again for several years."

"All that, and your mom is taking care of that woman willingly?"

"Gran came back and apologized for her behavior— but not for calling my mom a gold digger. I don't even know why she would think that. I mean, my parents have nice things now, but they've worked for every dime they have. Dad isn't rich by any means.

"But I remember that scene so well because I didn't know what that term meant. I thought it was so cool that Mom was a gold digger, I took my toy shovel to the backyard and dug holes everywhere, looking for my own gold. Anyway, Gran agreed to stop spewing her vitriol about their marriage when she showed up on our doorstep one day, so they let her back into our family. She kept her word for the most part, other than some occasional indirect remarks."

"Wow. Okay. So, when Hunter broke up with you, did you ask him about what she'd said?"

"No, I didn't. He used her words almost verbatim. We weren't right for each other. If we stayed together, we'd both regret it later. I'd find someone else and forget all about him. Everything had been fine between us just the day before, until he talked to Gran and listened to every word she said about me. He had every opportunity to explain what I'd heard and why he'd listened to her. But he didn't. He walked out of my house and my life forever."

"Not forever, Mal. He just walked into the restaurant and right back into your life tonight. Maybe this trip home will be your Christmas miracle on Main Street."

"You are such a dork. And why do you keep taking his

side? You're supposed to be *my* best friend." I sit down beside her and pull the pillow into my lap, hugging it to my chest.

"Mallory Alexandra Conner, I should wash your mouth out with soap for saying that. I have never and will never side with anyone over you. But you've barely dated anyone in the last four years I've known you. When some guy starts getting too close to you after a few dates, you find any reason under the sun to kick him to the curb."

"You're exaggerating, Meli."

"No, I'm not. Remember Russell? You broke up with him because he poured the milk in the bowl before the cereal."

"That was just weird, and you know it."

"And Grant? You quit seeing him because of his toes."

"Did you see his feet in sandals? His toes were like fingers! I can't handle finger-like toes."

"What about Ronnie? You didn't like the way he kissed."

"Noooo. He kissed just fine. It was the way he said 'yummy' after every kiss that I couldn't handle. Don't even try to tell me you'd put up with that for a week, much less a month."

"Okay, I'll give you that one. My point is you haven't exactly given another man a real chance to get to know you since Hunter. Maybe it's not that you want him back as much as you want closure—for both your relationship with him and your grandmother."

"So, you think I should confront him and demand answers while I'm here."

"That sounds a little…aggressive. Maybe approach it more as a friendly talk to restore an old friendship and clear the air."

"For the record, I like my plot of waterboarding, removing fingernails, and stringing him up by his balls better."

"Duly noted. Keep those ideas in your back pocket in case you need a Plan B."

We laugh together, and my mood lightens, the way it always does when my best friend puts my life back into perspective for me. "I feel sorry for everyone else in the world."

"Why is that?"

"Because I have the best friend ever, and they don't."

"You're not going to kiss me now, are you? That would just make things awkward. I've told you before, I love you, but not like that."

"Shut up."

"What did he say to you before we left the restaurant? I could tell he wanted a second alone with you, so I hung back a few steps to give you two a little privacy."

"But only long enough for you to get me alone later?" I give Amelia the side eye, playfully questioning her motives.

"Exactly. Now quit stalling and spill it."

"He didn't say anything significant. Dad had just said he finally understood why Mr. Kirkman refused to play Santa anymore, and Hunter had a good laugh about it. Then he looked at me and said I should start thinking about what I'll tell Santa I want for Christmas this year."

"Funny guy. Everyone thinks they're a comedian."

A knock on the door immediately brings a smile to Amelia's face. "That's your mom bringing hot chocolate with tiny marshmallows before tucking us into bed."

Who is this crazy person sitting beside me?

"Since when did you get in touch with your inner child?"

"Open the door, Mal. It's hot chocolate. With tiny marshmallows. Chop, chop. You're wasting time." She motions toward the door, clearly over her concern for my imaginary love life.

"Come on in, Mom." I take one of the cups from her and kiss her on the cheek. "Thank you for spoiling us."

"You are so welcome. And I would gladly spoil you more if you came home more often."

"Nice segue, Mom. Not obvious at all."

"While I'm at it, your father and I recently had a talk, and we agree we'd both love to have a few grandkids soon."

The hot chocolate gets stuck in my throat when I start nervously coughing. "Geez, Mom. That's not funny. I may need skin grafts on my esophagus now."

"Stop whining, Mallory. I'm still waiting for my hot chocolate." Amelia narrows her eyes at me, daring me to take any more of Mom's time.

"Here's yours, Amelia. I put extra marshmallows in it for you, sweetie. I remember that's how you liked it from our visit last Christmas."

"Thank you, Mama Jackie. This is perfect." Amelia puts on a good show of enjoying her drink—eyes closed, soft moans, and licking her lips. She's such a ham.

"Sweetheart, I'll be with Gran all day tomorrow, but when I get back, your dad and I will take you two girls out so we can show Amelia around our winter wonderland."

"Since I've seen it a time or two, why don't you take Amelia, and I'll stay here?"

"If you don't go with us, you can stay with Gran. Give her sitter a break."

"That's really cold, Mom."

"So is trying to get out of spending time with your family, while you're home to spend time with your family."

"Being logical is so overrated. Fine. I'll walk around town with you, in the freezing cold, with the horrible four-letter-word white precipitation all around us, and suffer through frostbitten fingers and toes."

"You know, you really should've been an actress instead of going to college for early childhood education. You're quite dramatic." Mom smiles sweetly, but I know it's secretly a smile of triumph. I'll choose the cold air of our little town over the cold heart of Gran any day.

"Everyone's a comedian these days. Usually at my expense."

"You just give us so much material." Amelia smirks at me over the rim of her mug. Then she shifts her gaze to my mom. "Hey, Mama Jackie. Since Mr. Kirkman retired, do you think it's safe for Mallory and me to sit in Santa's lap while we're here?"

"That can definitely be arranged. We've needed new Christmas pictures for a long time now. What a great idea, Amelia."

"Yes. Thank you, Amelia, for that suggestion. I appreciate it so much. Remind me to show you how much when Mom isn't around."

Amelia's smirk turns into a full belly laugh that she doesn't even try to hide.

"Mallory, behave. Amelia is our guest."

"Are you kidding right now, Mom?"

Mom smiles and pats my shoulder as she leaves the bedroom. When I turn my sights back to Amelia, she wiggles farther under the covers. "It's so cozy here."

"Yeah, I think you're getting a little too comfortable."

CHAPTER FOUR

Hunter

"How are you, Henry?" One of my carriage drivers arrives for work as I'm walking into the barn with a bale of hay.

"I'm good, Hunter. How's it going?" He lovingly strokes the large black Percheron chomping on the hay. The love and care he shows the horses make me think about how much Henry must miss his wife. She passed away several years ago, so he works part time giving tourists sleigh rides to pass the time.

"All good. Looks like it'll be a beautiful night for a sleigh ride."

"Sure does. There's snow on the ground around the lake, and the moon will be high in the sky. Perfect setting for all the lovebirds visiting us this year."

"Do you need any help getting this big guy hitched up before I leave for Santa's Village?"

"Nah, I'm fine. He's my buddy. We have our routine

down pat by now. Have fun on the guided ride with all the tourists."

I leave Henry with the sleigh horses and meet my best friend Chad outside the barn. He has the trail horses all saddled and ready to go. The six tourists in today's group are all from the same family, making my trip easier to manage. The kids will ride the most experienced trail horses in the middle of the pack, still tethered to the other horses to help keep them safe.

"Is everyone ready to go to Santa's Village and see what his elves are making today?" I ask loudly as I approach.

"Yeah!" the kids yell in unison while jumping up and down.

"Well, get on your horses so we can go! What are you waiting for?"

"Chad said we had to wait for you, Hunter!" The smallest girl of the group smiles up at me. Her front two teeth are missing, making her even cuter.

With her shiny chestnut hair and snaggle-tooth smile, she reminds me of another little girl I used to know.

Chad and I double-check the horses' tack before helping the family onto their assigned horses. I take the lead and Chad takes the rear as we set off up the mountain to Santa's Village. While my family has owned and oper-ated the horse sleigh rides around town for years, this is a new endeavor I started a couple of years ago. Even though the trail leads up the side of the mountain, it's wide open and an easy climb for the horses. The road leading up to my new business is actually more dangerous in the winter than the horse trail is.

Santa's Village is a year-round business, but the Christmas tourist season more than puts me in the black for the rest of the year. The Bavarian-themed buildings in the village are trimmed in small white lights. A large red sleigh stays parked right outside Santa's Workshop, the main store in the park, so he can load the toys onto it as the elves finish them. A corral with eight reindeer is nearby, complete with a feeding station for the guests to get up close and personal.

The outdoor ice-skating rink was an expensive addition but more than worth the investment. It's a miniature version of the outdoor rinks in several major cities that uses a special substance to keep the ice frozen at a consistent temperature all year. This specialized machinery opened up a whole new stream of revenue, especially when we started promoting Christmas in July at Santa's Village. Business has been booming ever since, and I've worked my ass off day and night to make that happen.

When we reach the village, the kids are more than ready to jump off the horses and right into Santa's lap. In this case, Santa is actually my dad, all dressed up and fluffed up in the middle. The line of kids waiting to tell Santa what they want for Christmas is long, and the first thing I notice about him is how he's squirming in his chair. His back must still be acting up because he keeps moving every few seconds, unable to find a comfortable position.

"Chad, do you think you can get one of the other guys to help you take the group back down the mountain? Looks like I'll have to help out Dad, after all."

He turns and watches Dad for a couple of minutes then shakes his head. "I know exactly where you get your stubborn streak from—and he's sitting right there. I'll grab one of the elves from the barn to ride your horse back down. Don't worry about us."

"Thanks, man. I appreciate it." With a pat on his

shoulder, I walk off toward Santa. "Hey, kids, we need to borrow Santa for a minute. We've had a change in the Naughty and Nice List in the back, and we need his approval. He'll be right back."

Dad stands and looks around at the kids who start to groan in protest. "I hope none of your names are now on the Naughty List." The groaning immediately stops, so Dad leaves the kids with his signature "Ho, ho, ho" laugh.

When we reach the back room, Dad removes the hat and beard. "Hey, Hunter. Is something wrong?"

"Yes, your back. You're in pain—I can tell by the way you're moving. You need to step out of the Santa suit and make an appointment with Dr. Kenrick. Let her help you get over this instead of just suffering through it."

"I know you're right. Denise is good at what she does. I'll make an appointment with her first thing in the morning."

"You're definitely hurting worse than you're admitting. You never willingly make an appointment with any kind of doctor. Take off the suit and give it to me. I'll finish out the night as Santa for you. Sneak out the back door and take some pain medicine when you get home."

After he sheds his costume, I throw it on and add extra stuffing to the middle before strolling out to Santa's chair. The kids in line are getting antsy, ready to share their list of wishes, get their picture taken, and eat their candy. One after the other, the little tots climb up on my lap, their parents snap quick pictures with their phones, while our photographer captures the professional photos. I listen intently as each child describes the most coveted toy of the week.

Then I hear her voice.

"Amelia, you have to be joking. We're not really sitting on Santa's lap!"

"Oh yes, we are. I'm telling Santa what I want for Christmas this year, and so are you. By the way, you want a man. It's been way too long, and you're extra cranky because of it. Or, rather, lack of it."

"Shut up." Mallory starts to turn away, but Amelia catches her arm. "Amelia, I'm too old for this."

The kid at the end of the line looks up at Mal. Though I can't see his face, I hear his little voice plain as day. "You're never too old to tell Santa what you want. How else will he know what to bring you for Christmas?"

She's trapped. She can't squash the dreams of a child by revealing the truth, so she's forced to play along. And wait in line behind him. Mallory Conner is waiting in line to sit on my lap. My focus shifts to her, intently watching and waiting, to the point I have to force myself to listen to the kids.

Finally. After hours and hours of waiting—or minutes, same difference—she's climbing the steps up the platform. A deep shade of crimson creeps up her neck and covers her face as she approaches. She refuses to meet my gaze, which is fine by me. That makes it less likely she'll recognize me and bolt. She didn't exactly give me a warm reception at dinner last night, although she seemed to tolerate my intrusion the longer we sat together. Thawing her heart won't be easy, but I'm more than willing to warm her up.

Mallory squeezes her eyes shut when she bends her knees and slides onto my knee. I almost laugh because she's barely touching me, holding most of her weight on her toes. The kids in line behind Amelia are pointing and giggling, but Amelia has zeroed in her focus on me. Recognition lights in her eyes and her lips part, as if she's about to reveal my ruse. Then she shuts her mouth just as quickly, and her lips curl into a satisfied smirk.

Mallory tries to stay as far away from me as possible while fulfilling her promise to tell Santa what she wants for Christmas. But we can't have that, can we? So, I wrap my arm around her waist and slide her across my leg until her body is flush against my chest. The old feelings stir deep inside, the same as they have every day since I lost her. Since I let her go. She feels soft yet firm, cold yet warm, near yet far.

"Would you like some sweeties, little girl?" I lean in close and whisper in her ear, mustering the best bedroom voice I have. "Now, tell Santa what you want, and I'll make sure you get it."

Her delayed reaction to my offer plays out like an animated character in a cartoon. It takes a few seconds before my words sink in, then her eyes grow wide. A couple more seconds and my voice registers, making her head swivel to look at me. Then her face contorts when she fully realizes who the man behind the beard is.

"Are you freaking kidding me right now? How dare you—"

"Now, now, little girl. That's no way to talk to Santa. Especially this close to Christmas and in front of all the little kids." I deepen my voice, allowing the bass to take over, and she clams up before she says something she can't take back.

"Well, *Santa*, let me tell you exactly what I expect to find in my stocking this year. I want a super-charged rabbit to help me achieve what no man ever has."

For the first time in my life, I'm shocked speechless. The kids within earshot, however, are not.

"Hey, I want a rabbit too!"

"Mom, can I have a rabbit?"

"Bunny rabbits! I love bunny rabbits!"

At least I have the benefit of a fake beard to hide my face behind. When Mallory meets the disapproving glares from the moms in the crowd, she tries to use her long brown hair to shield her face. But the heat emanating from it is hot enough to melt the snow around us.

"Well, little girl, you've caused quite a scene, as usual. In case you were wondering, that's not a rabbit in my pocket. I really am glad to see you."

"Just shoot me now. Seriously. Now I can never show my face in this town again."

"Ah, it's not that bad. Look on the bright side—things could be so much worse. We could go skinny-dipping in the hot tub, and you could show your ass instead."

"You know you're just making it harder, don't you?"

"No, babe, that's exactly what you're doing. Wiggle on my lap a little more, and we will make front page news."

She rolls her eyes and suppresses a laugh, something I'd love to hear her do again. The last time she laughed with me was just before we broke up—a long time ago now. After that day, her smile faded and her laughter disappeared…at least as far as I'm concerned.

"You and I are old news, Santa. No one cares about yesterday anymore. Just make sure you get my toy right."

She leaves the platform, bouncing down the steps like she doesn't have a care in the world, and heads toward Santa's Workshop. I feel someone else slide onto my lap before I can tear my eyes away from Mallory. When I turn to my next visitor, I expect to see a small child, but find Amelia's intense stare on me instead.

"Santa, I want my best friend to be happy again. And I want the man who broke her heart to do whatever it takes to put the pieces back together again. Or else, no one will ever find all the pieces of said heartbreaker after I'm through with him. We understand each other, yes?"

"Absolutely."

I don't scare easily, but Amelia has a mean streak hidden under that charming Southern exterior. She follows up with a sweet smile, as if she didn't just threaten me within an inch of my life, before she abruptly stands. "I'm glad we understand each other. The clock is ticking, Santa. You'd better break out the mistletoe and all the things that sparkle to impress my girl."

CHAPTER FIVE

Mallory

As I walk around Santa's Workshop, the scene with Hunter replays in my mind like a scene from a movie set to loop endlessly. I don't want to feel what I'm feeling right now. The way his arm felt around my waist. The warmth of his breath against my cheek. How the low-pitch of his voice vibrated against the shell of my ear when he whispered sexy nothings to me. This is insane—I'm insane.

After all this time apart.

After the pain and humiliation he caused me when we split up.

After I swore him off forever.

Just because he shows me the slightest bit of attention, I'm like an inexperienced young girl falling for him all over again.

"Well, you certainly had an interesting visit with Santa. Why on earth did we wait so long to visit this awesome place?" Amelia sidles up next to me, her face intentionally passive. But I know my best friend, and she's anything but passive.

"What did you do, Amelia?"

"Nothing. Nothing at all. What are you talking about?"

"Uh-huh. It'll come out. It always does."

"In this case, I hope you're right." She turns on her high-beam smile and walks over to examine a display case of Christmas goodies, leaving me with no real answers.

The smell of fresh-brewed coffee hits me, nearly making me salivate right where I stand. I follow the rich aroma to the back of the store and find the counter. The pastries in the case immediately draw my attention. "Are these from Myles Coffee Company in town?"

"Yes, they are. Would you like one?" The cute little barista in the elf outfit and matching apron steps toward me.

"Yes, I do. I can't resist them." I point to the biggest one they have and order a large white chocolate mocha to go with it. The people at the table closest to the fireplace leave just in time for me to grab the most coveted seat.

The garland on the mantel is professionally decorated with the biggest sphere- and teardrop-shaped ornaments I've ever seen, in an assortment of green, gold, and red. A shimmery red tulle twines over and under the trimmings, tying them together. Tiny white lights twinkle within the fabric, sending starbursts through the mesh. On the wall above the mantel hangs a hand-painted picture of Santa and one of his reindeer, and three wreaths made of mistletoe and red bows flank it on both sides.

Looking around the shop, I notice all the other unassuming special touches that make the business as cozy as it can be. Pictures of locals playing in the snow, riding in the sleighs, and singing Christmas carols are strategically placed amid similarly themed decorations. Colorful hand-painted signs with whimsical quotes draw my attention next.

And that's when I see it. I rise from my seat and walk to the table full of romantic Christmas decorations, forgetting my pastry and coffee are unfinished.

The wooden keepsake box I ordered specially made for Hunter years ago, with both of our names and a promise of a forever love carved into the lid, is in a prominent place amid the true-love-themed collection. I reach out to touch it, running my fingers along the words while the memories run through my mind.

"It's beautiful, isn't it?" I turn to find a young girl in an elf costume. Her name tag reads Nadine. She can't be more than seventeen, if that old.

"Yes, it is."

"It's not for sale, though, in case you were wondering. Mr. Beckett won't part with it, even though several people have asked to buy it."

"*Mr. Beckett* won't part with it?" I'm so confused. Did Hunter's father donate this box to the store? And why would he care about a gift from his son's girlfriend from when we were teenagers?

"No. He won't even consider it." She chuckles and shakes her head. "But we can engrave a new one for you if you'd like."

"No, thank you. I'm just looking." I walk back to my fireside table and absently sip on what's left of my coffee, still feeling perplexed.

"Want to tell me what that forlorn expression is all about?"

I look up and find Amelia sitting across from me. Funny thing, I didn't even hear her approach. "Did you really just say 'forlorn'? Does anyone actually use that word in everyday conversation?"

"Only when they're attempting to be over-the-top dramatic and make a very poignant point."

"Ah. I suppose 'poignant point' is in the same category with 'forlorn,' huh?"

"Absolutely. And when you try to get out of answering my very direct questions, you dodge and deflect or evade and misdirect. I'm onto you, though, missy. So, let's hear it."

Knowing she won't stop until I spill everything, I recount the entire scene of finding the engraved box and admit I can't make sense out of any of it. Then she stares at me—with her *you've-got-to-be-kidding-me* expression firmly set on her face.

"Mallory, with all sincerity, you're one of the smartest people I know. But right now, you're just being plain stupid."

"Look, I know what you're going to say. Believe me, out of the million thoughts running through my mind, at least one of the scenarios is that Hunter still has feelings for me. And maybe he does—but who's to say it's not just one of nostalgia? It's been four years since we were together, Meli. Time has a way of romanticizing the past, making it seem better than it really was. The fact of the matter is, I haven't heard from him in all that time. Not once. And after the way we parted, how can I believe anything but what I see?"

"What do you see, Mal?"

"We were young—too young for the strong feelings we had for each other. Maybe he has fond memories of us, but that doesn't mean instant happily ever after. That means

I'll be the girl he used to know when he tells his wife about me one day."

"You are way too young to be so cynical. We'll have to work on that. It's really not an attractive quality."

"Bite me."

"I'm really going to enjoy saying 'I told you so' one day very soon."

"You should get a cup of coffee and one of the pastries in that case up there. They're delicious. When you nearly have an orgasm from the combination, I'll be able to say 'I told you so' tonight."

When she returns with her food and coffee, she slides into the seat and shocks the hell out of me. "What'd you tell Santa you wanted for Christmas? Coffee and pastries? Or more orgasms? I'm curious."

When I raise my eyes to meet hers, I immediately realize she knows who was under the fake beard and the large red suit. So much for flying under the radar with the whole sitting-on-my-ex's-lap thing.

"I definitely went with more orgasms. Didn't you hear us? The rest of the line did."

Not expecting that answer from me, she spews hot coffee across the table before choking on the small amount she was in the middle of swallowing. "Actually, no, I didn't. I was distracted by this extremely handsome man waiting in line with his niece."

"Oh good, we can finally talk about your lack of love life instead of mine."

"Uh, no, we can't. Yours needs more immediate attention. Besides, you haven't told me what everyone else in line overheard you saying to Hunter."

One humiliation per night should be the legal limit, but it seems I'm shit out of luck in that department. After recounting my embarrassing gaffe—and enduring Amelia's fit of laughter—all eyes are on us again.

"Where has this Mallory been the last four years? We missed getting into so much trouble together."

"This town just seems to bring it out in me."

"Sounds to me like Hunter is the one who brings it out of you."

"Without a doubt, it's all Hunter's fault."

"What am I getting credit for this time?" Hunter pulls out the extra chair from the table and makes himself comfortable.

"Credit? No, Hunter, you're getting all the blame." Amelia laughs and pops a piece of her cinnamon bun in her mouth.

"Credit. Blame. Semantics. All depends on how good the story is."

"This is all about your bad influence skills over my best friend. I'm really enjoying it, to be honest. Maybe you should share some pointers."

"I wish I could take credit for it—but the truth is, that's just who she is. I think she's just more comfortable showing that side when I'm around." Hunter smirks with his sexy, half grin, knowing damn well that was the smile I never could resist.

"We both know that someone had to take the blame for all the trouble we got into. That someone was just usually me."

Even though I want to hate him, I can't. Not when I'm around him. His easygoing personality disarms me every time. He's the perfect combination of laid-back and high-strung. How he pulls that off is a mystery to me and always has been. But he does it so well. His outer demeanor is cool and calm, but I can sense the pent-up energy just below the surface. Like a panther ready to pounce on its unsuspecting prey. Only now, I'm very suspicious and on constant alert where he's concerned. He's pouring on the charm and saying all the right things. Bringing up the best memories. Making our reunion feel like it was planned instead of purely coincidental.

He's talking, carrying most of the conversation as he regales Amelia with tales of our high school exploits. For added emphasis, he cuts his eyes to me at pivotal moments, keeping that live wire between us fully energized. I don't even know what he's talking about because his lips are all I can focus on at the moment. Full and soft, yet hot and demanding when they were against my skin. I mean, the mistletoe is right there on the wall above our heads. Perfect excuse.

When I told Amelia he was my first, I didn't elaborate. He was my first everything. My first best friend. My first partner in crime. My first crush. My first kiss. My first love. My first lover. Everything I learned about love in the first degree was with him. The problem was, at eighteen years old, I believed he was my whole life, my future, my everything. Finding out the truth was beyond painful.

But knowing my own grandmother was the driving force behind our breakup knocked me to my knees. Knowing Hunter agreed with what she said about me sent me into a deep, dark tailspin I'm not sure I've recovered from yet. Sometimes I wish I'd never overheard that conversation, so I'd be none the wiser. But at times like now, when I find myself being pulled back under his spell, wishing I could kiss those perfect lips of his just one more time, reliving that moment brings me back to my senses.

"Do you know a man named Chad with the cutest three-year-old niece you've ever seen? Her name is

Lauren." Amelia tries to act nonchalant, as if she's making casual conversation. But I know her better than she thinks I do. Chad made quite an impression on her.

"Yes, I know him very well. Chad Sanders. We've been friends forever, and we work together now. I'm sure Mallory remembers him. How do you know him?"

"I don't really. We met while standing in line to see Santa tonight and talked for a few minutes. He seems like a good guy." Amelia glances around the store, refusing to make eye contact with me now that I've tuned back into the conversation.

"Is he still single?" I get straight to the point Amelia has only been hinting at. Her gaze slides back to mine, the muscles around her eyes crinkling as she narrows them at me.

Hunter doesn't want to answer me at first, showing the first sign of insecurity I've ever seen out of him. He thinks I'm interested in Chad. "Um, yeah, he is. No wife. No girlfriend. Just a younger sister he guards with his life and a niece who hung the moon and stars in his eyes."

"He did dote on her more than most guys I've seen. I thought she was his daughter at first." Amelia leans in to engage and gain more information on Chad.

"Lauren's dad took off when Tara was still pregnant. Chad looked for Brett for weeks, but it's a good thing Chad never found him. He was out for blood. He assumed the responsibility for taking care of those two little ladies from that day on."

"What about Tara's parents? Do they help too?"

"Not so much. They weren't too happy with her when she came home pregnant at seventeen and told them her baby's daddy was almost twice her age."

"She was barely legal. I don't blame them for being

mad at Brett, but Tara and Lauren still needed them." When Amelia finds a cause, she latches on with both hands. Her sudden and severe change in tone is potentially worrisome. Crusade against injustice is on her business card.

"Believe me, Chad has more than made up for his parents' lack of involvement. And he's told them several times what he thinks about it. He's one of the good guys. Maybe I should set you two up, then you can tag-team their parents and give them hell."

"Hmm." Amelia pretends to consider his offer. We both know she's interested. "Maybe you should."

"A double date would probably be best. You know, to help break the ice and ease the awkwardness of a first date. Don't you think, Mal?" Hunter looks at me, but there's no humor in his eyes. What I see is pure desire, and it sets me on fire all the way to my core.

No way around it…I'm doomed.

CHAPTER SIX

Hunter

"A double date? You may have the right idea, Hunter. I'm sure there's a hot, single man left in this little town. Not a tourist, though. They're here with their families, and that would just be weird." Mallory taps her pursed lips with her manicured fingertip, pretending to give the idea serious consideration.

She thinks she's so funny. Okay, usually she is, but she also knows exactly how to push my buttons and make me instantly jealous of a fictional man. She has no intentions of finding some random guy to take on a double date, but she does want to make me squirm until the very last second. I can take it, though. But I wonder…can she?

"Sure, there are still plenty of single men here. You know most of them from school. In fact, I saw the perfect man for you just now, walking around in Santa's Village, on my way in here."

The cute little smirk on her face fades, and a leery expression takes its place. "Who would that be?"

"You remember Ian Butler, right? I'm sure he'd jump at the chance to take you out. In fact, I can go outside and try to find him right now." To prove my point, I start to stand, but she reaches across the table and grabs my arm to stop me.

"No, no, no, no, no. Don't do that. I'm friends with him on Facebook, and he's been shopping around for a wife for a while now. He'll get the wrong idea. Besides, he has that whole toenail fungus problem going on. I wouldn't be able to think of anything except wondering how he'd ever get a pedicure without an electric grinder on hand."

Amelia's laugh escapes before she can stop it. She quickly tries to cover it with a cough, but that only makes her sound like she's choking. I reach over and pat her on the back, feigning concern over her sudden outburst. "Are you okay, Amelia?"

"Fine. Fine. Don't worry about me. Let's just find Mallory a date and hope Chad is interested in one with me." She covers her mouth with her hand, but that does little to hide her mile-wide smile.

"Oh, I know. What about Leon Bolt? He has his own business and owns a whole fleet of cars."

"Now you're not even trying. He took over the funeral home from his parents so they could travel, and his fleet of cars is actually hearses. The one he drives everywhere has a magnetic sign on the side, advertising his business. His funeral home business, Hunter. That's just creepy. He also went through that period where he thought he was a vampire. At least until he walked in on an embalming in process and passed out cold when he saw the blood."

"That's true. He still doesn't oversee that part of the business to this day. He stays upstairs and handles the sales. But he's very successful."

"How is he very successful? Has there been a rash of deaths in the last four years I don't know about?"

"No, nothing macabre like that. He started a side business and apparently makes a killing at it."

"Doing what?"

Amelia's eyes follow the conversation between us like she's watching a tennis match at Wimbledon. The urge to smile is killing me, but I keep my expression neutral.

"He's an Uber driver."

"You're shitting me right now."

"I'm dead serious."

"He doesn't use the hearse to pick up fares, does he?"

"Yes, of course, he does. Have you seen how much room they have in the back of those cars? An entire family's luggage will fit back there. Plus, he has the funeral home limo that he uses for special occasions—weddings, proms, stuff like that."

"Leon Bolt is a big fat no. I'm not going on a date in a hearse or a funeral limo. That's just wrong."

Amelia's purse slips off the back of her chair, with a little help from Amelia herself, and she leans over to pick it up. Even with her face hidden under the table, I can still see her shoulders jumping and hear her muffled snickers. Mallory doesn't notice how long it takes Amelia to retrieve her purse because she's so engrossed in the mental images of Ubering via hearse. I lift my coffee to my lips and enjoy a good, long drink, not even bothering to hide my smile. Neither of my table mates is looking at me anyway.

When Amelia finally rights herself, her face is bright red and tears shimmer in her eyes. She dabs one corner with her napkin and takes a deep breath to calm herself. The scene is a lot like having a funny thought stuck in your head while in the middle of a quiet church sermon. The harder you try to control yourself, the worse you make the situation for both yourself and everyone around you. Amelia finally makes eye contact with me, only to be overcome by yet another snigger.

"Excuse me. My coffee must've gone down the wrong way." She pats her chest, playing off her ruse with expert skill. We both know she's full of shit, but whatever. We'll both pretend we don't know the truth of what just happened anyway. "As fun as it's been to try to choose a date for Mallory, can I make a suggestion?"

"I'm listening." I tilt my head to the side, curious to hear where she'll go with this. Mallory looks at her friend and nods, though she's still slightly disturbed by Leon's side-business dealings.

"Mallory, the only logical choice for your date is Hunter. He's friends with Chad. He's already going to talk to Chad on my behalf. It would be weird if Hunter did all the work, only for you to show up with Leon."

"Makes sense to me. Mal, you okay with this plan?"

"Um, yeah, sure. I can't…I can't show up with Leon."

"It's settled, then. Tomorrow night good with you two ladies?"

"Tomorrow night is perfect, Hunter. Give me your phone, and I'll text my cell to you. All you have to do is let me know what time, and I'll make sure Mallory is ready to go."

I hand my phone over to Amelia, but Mallory is the one who holds my attention. Thoughts of Leon and hearses are leaving her mind, while memories of her and me take their place. The slight twinge of sadness in her eyes gives away her thoughts. No, wait—it's not sadness. It's fear. Fear of being with me again. Fear of allowing herself to both face the past and face the future. I'm not sure which emotion is worse. Either way, my plan to erase all the bad times and remind her of the good times is underway. And the clock is ticking, because she'll be gone again in just a couple of weeks.

"My break is over. Time to get back to playing Santa—the kids are waiting. And I'll be impatiently waiting for tomorrow night. See you then, beautiful."

"Good night, Santa. Don't forget to call Chad."

On my way to change clothes, I do just that. "Hey man, we have a double date tomorrow night. Here's the plan."

AFTER A FEW RAPS ON THE DOOR, I STEP BACK AND WAIT, holding my breath to see if Mallory actually answers. She may have headed back to Georgia in the middle of the night just to avoid our forced double date tonight. Little does she know, that won't stop me. I'll just follow her back to Athens, and we'll have our date Southern-style, to match her new accent. There's no way I can right all the wrongs between us while we're nearly a thousand miles apart.

Pete answers the door wearing a smug grin. After a firm handshake, he invites us in. "I'm sure I don't have to tell you boys this, but the girls are still getting ready. And they've been bickering the entire time. Mallory says Amelia stole her shirt. Amelia says it's always been her shirt, and Mallory only claims it because she kept it so long after she borrowed it."

"They sound like sisters." Chad chuckles, knowing too well what that's like.

"You're exactly right—they're sisters in nearly every sense of the word. Jackie and I have all but legally adopted

Amelia as our own. You two are brave to take them on a double date. You won't have a dull moment tonight, that's for sure." Pete tells us to take a seat while we wait for the girls to finish dressing.

We make small talk, chatting about the number of visitors, the Christmas forecast, and how the family is doing. But I know Pete has more to say to me—something too personal to say in front of Chad. He seriously considers it a couple of times, then changes his mind again. After Mallory and I broke up, I have no idea what she told her parents happened. No matter what I did in an attempt to make her to talk to me, to be my friend again at the very least, she wouldn't hear it. Pete and Jackie never treated me any differently, but I'm sure they resented me for their only daughter's broken heart and choice of out-of-state college.

The girls make their grand entrance just in time, since I'm sure Pete was about to throw caution to the wind and say exactly what has been on his mind immediately before we heard their voices coming from the stairs.

"In case you've forgotten, this is all your fault anyway. You should give me the shirt as payment for interrupting my plans." Mallory is arguing her case, whatever that may be.

"Interrupting your plans? You need to step away from the crack pipe, girl. Your only plans were to find the bottom of the Ben & Jerry's container while watching sappy Lifetime movies in your pajamas. If anything, you should buy me a new shirt for making you leave the house." Amelia fires her own jabs back at Mallory.

"Crack pipe? You're the one who needs to quit hitting the crack pipe. I leave the house all the time—I'm leaving tonight! But what you signed me up for is just wrong. Wrong, Amelia!"

"Stop being a baby. It's time to put on your big-girl panties and deal with life. I'm telling you this as your best friend."

"I'd prefer you stop being such a good friend to me, then."

They turn the corner and walk into the den where we're waiting, unfazed by our presence and our over-hearing their quarrel.

"What's the plan for tonight, fellas?" Amelia asks, her Southern twang bleeding through her words more than usual.

"Dinner and a show." My reply is technically correct—just possibly not in the same manner they're expecting. Variety is the spice of life and all that bullshit. Right?

"Sounds great. We're ready to go." Amelia turns to Pete and hugs his neck. "Don't worry about us, Dad. We'll be back before you even realize we're gone."

"Have fun. Call me if you need anything."

"Thank you, Daddy. Love you." Mallory hugs him next then moves to stand beside me, though she's just far enough away to avoid touching me.

"Love you, too, jelly bean." Ah, the pet name he always used for her. That should create a sense of nostalgia in her.

"Dad." She pretends to complain, but she secretly loves the way he dotes on her.

Amelia and Chad are already waiting at the door, having a private conversation and completely ignoring the rest of us. Seems this date is working out for half of us anyway. I slide my hand down Mallory's arm and lace our fingers together. She stares at our linked hands in surprise, but she doesn't try to pull away from me. That's a good sign.

"Ready to go, Mal? We're having dinner and drinks at The Cove before the show. Our table is waiting."

The chatter in my truck on the way to the best bar in town is warm and friendly, from everyone. We've talked enough about the past; now I'm learning all about their present. Their life in Athens, their time in college, and the adventures they've had. Amelia still swears Mallory isn't the same person I've described, but she feels the same to me.

Once we're seated inside the bar, the owner stops by our table to say hello.

"Grey McDaniels! I haven't seen you in forever!" Mallory stands and embraces Grey.

"Well, if you'd get your skinny ass home more often, you'd see me all the time. Did you lose your passport or something?"

"I'm only in Georgia, Grey."

"Yeah, I know. Don't you need a passport to come back home from there, or do they just let anyone back into the state?"

"Ha-ha. You're still so funny. Say hello to your brother for me."

"Hang around for a while, and you may get to say hello yourself. Roan's coming home for Christmas this year."

"A big-time country music star back in our little town? Don't let the tourists overhear that news!"

"He'll be secluded enough at the cabin, but you know you're always welcome to drop by and see us."

"I wouldn't crash your family Christmas, but if I just happen to be in the neighborhood…"

"Anytime, girl. Anytime."

Grey disappears back behind the bar, and our waitress stops to take our orders. We chat and laugh over the appetizers and drinks, with Mallory loosening up more and more with each sip. Not long after our meals arrive, she's joking and teasing everyone as if she'd never changed. As if she'd never left. Just like old times.

"What is this big show you keep talking about?" Mallory finally addresses me individually, ignoring the other couple who are completely into each other.

"I can't wait for you to see, but it has to be a surprise."

"I'm ready whenever you are."

Is it wrong that I really hope she means she's ready for more than just the show?

CHAPTER SEVEN

Mallory

W hen the idea of a double date was first mentioned, I was determined not to go. But the more I thought about it, the more it made sense. Coffee in Santa's Workshop was fine, just two old friends catching up. But a real date is just what I need to remind myself why we're not compatible. I realized Amelia was right about me during our "find Mallory a date" conversation, but not for the reason she thinks. Every guy I've gone out with was a terrible fit for me—that's why I couldn't get past even the minor annoyances. The men Hunter suggested were also horrible matches—and he knew that—but the trivial things I found wrong with those guys only confirmed my suspicions.

Trivial, except the Uber hearse thing. I just can't.

I haven't met my soul mate yet.

He's out there, but he's not anyone I've met yet. If he were, I'd already know.

So, that fact actually made my mind up for me. Go out

with Hunter, show him and Amelia once and for all I've moved past our juvenile relationship, and part on better terms this time. No unresolved feelings, no unearthed secrets, and no living in the past.

We leave from dinner and drinks at The Cove, and Hunter drives east out of town, so I immediately think we're going to the lake. But it's not cold enough yet for it to be frozen solid, so there's not much point of going there at night. Then I realize he has other plans when we turn north and head toward the mountain. I chance a glance over at him, the soft glow of the dash lights illuminating his face. Feeling my eyes on him, he turns his head in my direction. Even away from the lights of town, riding in his truck under the dark skies with bright twinkling stars, I can read his expression. I can hear his thoughts. I can feel the weight of his stare like fingertips caressing my skin.

"Penny for your thoughts, Snagglepuss." His lips curl up in a triumphant smile when my bottom jaw drops to my lap.

"Oh. My. God. I can't believe you brought up *that* nickname out of all the little pet names you've had for me over the years. I'd forgotten all about it, thankfully."

"Are you kidding? I'll never forget it. I'm sure I can still dig up your first-grade picture and remind you how you got that name."

"No. That's not necessary. All kids lose their baby teeth. I don't know why I got a special name to commemorate the childhood rite of passage."

"You don't know why? Really?"

"No, I have no idea. Tell me."

"Because even without your front teeth, you were the cutest girl in the whole school. You're just special, Mal."

"Yes. Snagglepuss does make me feel extra special. Really."

Hunter laughs at my sardonic reply, his rich, deep chuckle resonating in the cab. "It should make you feel special. You're the only one I've given that name to—that makes you one of a kind."

"With good reason. Everyone else calls it snaggle-tooth…not snaggle-puss."

"Tomato. To-mah-to. Same difference."

"Your reasoning skills blow my mind, Hunter. They're not even remotely close."

His reply to my argument is the same as it's always been—a hearty laugh at my expense. But for whatever reason, it makes me feel warm and fuzzy inside.

That shit needs to stop.

Halfway up the mountain, he turns into the parking area for Santa's Village. The place is deserted at this time of night since the kids are all tucked into their beds by now. The thousands of twinkling lights are off, and the entry gates are locked.

"What are we doing here? The park is closed, and all the businesses are dark." I'm positive he can see the confusion across my face and hear it in my voice.

"Yes, everything here is closed, because it's after hours. And that's exactly why we're here."

He hops out of the truck and walks around to open my door, taking my hand as I slide out of the plush leather seat. From the corner of my eye, I see Chad doing the same for Amelia, but the warmth of Hunter's hand wrapped around mine distracts me.

"If you get me arrested for trespassing, Hunter Beckett, I will kick your ass. Chief Land will keep me in the city jail just out of spite and show my mug shot during his scared straight visits at the high school."

"Stop worrying, Snagglepuss. I'll take care of you if Chief Land shows up again."

"We're not skinny-dipping tonight, Hunter. I mean it."

"It *is* a little too cold for that tonight. Maybe we'll visit the lake this summer and avoid getting caught then. For now, I have other plans, Mal."

Amelia and Chad appear to be in their own little world —and that world only has the two of them in it. Her arm is wrapped around his elbow, she's glued to his side, and even their footsteps are in cadence. She's not questioning why we're here. I doubt she has even looked around to see where we are. Right now, she only has eyes for Chad. I have a feeling I'm going home alone tonight.

When we reach the gates, Hunter unlocks them with a key from his pocket. I take a step backward and look from the lock to his face a couple of times. "Where did you get that key?"

"I'm Santa, remember?"

"If you say so." Okay, so that makes a little sense. He'd need access to the place to get dressed before the kids see him. But I doubt the Santa at Macy's gets his own store key, much less a key to the entire mall. "You know Chief Land still hates me, right?"

We're so getting arrested tonight.

He swings the metal gate open and motions for me to enter first. With only a slight hesitation, I step through the opening and release my held breath. At least we'll all go to jail together. When I turn toward Hunter again, he's locking the gate behind us. Is it odd that makes me feel safe? I mean, if I can't get out, Chief Land can't get in.

Hunter wraps his hand around mine again, and we

stroll along the deserted footpath, heading toward the very back of the complex.

"This place is amazing. I can't believe my parents didn't tell me about it. It literally makes me feel like I'm at the North Pole, walking through Santa's hometown."

"That's the idea. It definitely goes with the theme of the town, but this gives us the opportunity to offer the tourists more choices."

We stop in front of a small, outdoor ice-skating rink that I didn't even see yesterday. Hunter asks for everyone's shoe sizes before disappearing inside to get our skates. When he returns, I'm so excited to lace mine up and hit the ice, I can hardly wait.

"Do they not have ice-skating in Georgia?" Hunter smiles, pleased with himself.

"Yes, there are ice rinks, but they're all indoors. I miss skating on the lake in the dead of winter, but this outdoor rink will work every bit as well. There's just something about gliding across the ice underneath the stars."

"I know exactly what you mean." Hunter squeezes my hand, and we rise together from the bench.

"Chad, honey, I'll probably have to hold on to you for the first twenty or so passes until I get the hang of this. I grew up on roller blades, not ice blades." Amelia's excuse to stay close to Chad is a valid one—not that either of them seems to mind either way.

Hunter and I step onto the ice, and I'm instantly transported back in time to the cold winter nights when we skated together by the light of the moon. Most of the time, our lips and bodies stayed glued together, only moving our feet enough to continue the forward momentum. Even tonight, I can still feel his arms locked around my waist, his lips on mine, and the taste of him on my tongue. Sometimes, I miss those moments more than anything else—being so completely lost in someone that nothing else mattered.

Not school.

Not grades.

Not my future.

Just him.

When I feel his arms slide around my waist from behind, I instinctively lean back against his chest. Force of habit, maybe. Muscle memory, perhaps. Too long without sex, definitely. The man feels too damn good. And he smells too damn good. And he looks too damn good. And if I go to jail tonight, this still would be so damn worth it.

"You remember, don't you?" His lips brush the shell of my ear. The chills running down my arm have nothing to do with the cold night air. "How it feels to be in my arms. My lips against your bare skin. All the ways my tongue made you crazy. You remember everything about us, don't you?"

"How could I ever forget, Hunter?" My whispered reply doesn't make it any less true.

"Let's see if you remember how to skate doubles." He turns me around, keeping one arm around my waist for support.

We begin to move in tandem lap after lap, our actions as synchronized as professional skaters. At least, in my mind.

Until my blade catches on a gash in the ice.

The rest of our movements aren't so graceful. Even though I see them happening in slow motion, there's not a damn thing I can do to stop them. Since I was skating backward and holding on to Hunter, my body doesn't stop when my blade does. My arms are locked around Hunter's neck, and my grip tightens when I lose my balance, pulling him down with me. On top of me. As I fall flat on my back.

"There are much better ways of getting me on top of you, but you get points for creativity." His flirty smile would normally melt the thick layer of ice around my heart, but I have a much more pressing issue to deal with first.

As if I'm not humiliated enough already, my uncoordinated landing knocks the breath out of me. So while Hunter lies on top of me, trying to untangle himself without hurting me, I start barking like a seal, trying to remind my body how to breathe again. He rolls to my side but doesn't get up off the ice.

"Calm down. Just relax. Don't fight it, and it'll stop sooner." When my normal breathing resumes again, he smiles down at me. "There's never a dull moment with you around."

When we're both back on our feet again, I notice the concerned expression on Amelia's face and the amused one on Chad's. "I'm fine, Meli. Just watch for that crater in the ice on your next pass."

Undeterred after that unfortunate incident, we keep skating together, although now we're both facing forward and watching for nicks in the ice. When the moon is high in the sky and the snow starts to fall again, Hunter steers me to the exit.

"It's time for the next surprise."

"I'm not sure I'll survive any more surprises tonight." I laugh at my clumsiness, knowing I'm not hurt. I've fallen on the ice too many times in my life for this one to be any different.

We leave through the back entrance of the park—the

one next to the horse stables. There, drenched in moon-light and waiting in the deepest part of the snow, are two horse-drawn sleighs.

"Hunter, this is perfect. It's been so long since I've been on a sleigh ride."

"Let me help you in." Once we're seated, he unfolds the blanket and spreads it across our legs. Then he reaches down below the seat and pulls out an insulated mug and hands it to me. "This hot chocolate will help warm you."

The velvety smooth liquid slides down my throat as easily as the sleigh rails slide across the snow beneath us. Amelia and Chad are in the cart behind us, so our only company is the driver with his back to us. The snow starts to come down harder, but the moon still shines brightly through the scattered clouds to light the path. We really are riding in a winter wonderland, and I find myself naturally gravitating closer to Hunter. The wind blowing in our faces is cold, but we snuggle under the blanket well inside the carriage, taking turns with the thermos until the last drop is gone.

The large draft horse pulls us with no effort at all, over hills and around curves. Everything is quiet except the sound of his hooves striking the snow and his occasional snort. The woods are comforting and inviting, almost as much as the arms of the man beside me. For a moment, I get lost in a memory of him and me, how strong our love once was. It hits me how much of a hold he obviously still has over me.

Without even realizing it, I relax into him, my cheek presses against his chest, and his arms wrap around me. I feel his lips on the top of my head. Then they move lower, closer to my temple, because I've lifted my head to meet him. Then on my cheekbone, just below my eye. If I lift my face a little bit more, our lips will touch. If I completely give in and relax the rigid control I've held on to since the day I left Cringle Cove, I'll have the one thing I've craved the most but denied the hardest.

But I close my eyes and lower my head back to his chest instead. I've been here before—lost in Hunter, blinded by love and eventually jilted by it too. That's one place and time I never want to visit again. My moment of weakness passes. The beauty and allure of this town and this man are working hard to pull me back in, but I'm stronger than I used to be. I left it all behind once before. I can do it again.

With a glance down at my watch as I sit up, I make a show of checking the time. "It's getting late, and Amelia and I have to get up early tomorrow to help Dad in the clinic. I'm sorry to end this perfect night, but we really should be getting back."

Hunter nods, but he's not fooled. Not that I was trying to fool him—I've made my stance clear, except that momentary lapse in judgment. "Of course. Wouldn't want you to get in trouble for being late on your first day on the job, would we?"

"Very funny. Dad has enough going on right now. I'd feel bad if I overslept and caused him more trouble."

His expression turns serious. "How is your Gran doing, Mal? How's your dad holding up?"

"Uh, he's fine. Gran only had hernia surgery, so she's basically fine—just a little sore. That surgery is robotic-assisted now, which isn't a big deal at all. Mom's only helping her because she's old and shouldn't drive for a few days. And because she's a demanding, hateful old woman who expects everyone to cater to her every whim."

"Oh, okay. Are you going by to see her while you're home?"

"I had no intentions of seeing her, but my best friend in the whole wide world volunteered us to take over one day to give Mom a break. Not that I don't want to help my mom, but I'd rather do *anything* else. That's what we were arguing about when you and Chad arrived tonight."

"It's only for one day. Maybe you'll be glad you went."

"Yeah, I doubt that. At least Amelia will be with me, though, so I won't be the only one to suffer."

The trail loops back around to the spot where we started, and soon we're heading back down the mountain road to town. Conversation in the truck revolves around what a great night this has been—mainly from Amelia and Chad. Hunter and I chime in to keep the awkwardness to a minimum, but we both know it's there regardless of our acting abilities.

I've already made a similar decision about Hunter that I did about Gran.

Only one day with her. Only one date with him.

At the end of our break, my time in this town will come to an end. For good.

CHAPTER EIGHT

Hunter

"Have you heard back from Mallory?" Chad hoists the saddle onto his horse's back and begins securing it. He doesn't look at me, though, because he's trying to act casual.

"No, not a word. I've left her a voice mail and sent her a text—just in case. She hasn't answered either of them. That was three days ago." In fact, I haven't talked to her at all since I dropped her off after our date.

"Give her time and some space, man. She'll come around."

"Chad, she's had four years and nearly a thousand miles. I think she's had plenty of time and space from me."

"Well, when you put it that way…"

"Shut up and ride off into the sunset already. You have a group ride waiting for you." I hear him laugh as I leave the barn and walk toward the office. There's no point in asking if he's talked to Amelia. If I had to guess, which I don't even want to, she's the one he's been texting nonstop for the last few days.

"Good morning, Hunter." Mom's already at her desk, checking the schedules and confirming the payments for the upcoming reservations. I don't know what I'd do without her bookkeeping skills because I certainly can't do it all by myself. "You boys have a full day today."

"Yes, we do. You keep piling the tourists on us, one family after the other. Not that I'm complaining, though." She hands the day's full schedule to me, and I release a low whistle. "It's a good thing we all love our jobs because we won't be taking off anytime soon. We have more carriage and trail rides today than I thought."

"Don't stress over it. I've already talked to our extra trail guides, and they're on their way in as we speak. The horses will be tacked, and the riders will be in good hands."

"You're the best office manager ever, Mom. Thank you."

"No need to thank me. You're not the only one who loves their job."

"Did you manage to talk Henry into accepting his bonus? I'm glad he enjoys taking people out on sleigh rides, but he won't accept tips from the locals."

"Actually, I didn't tell him anything about it. It's automatically deposited into his account, so he won't even realize it until he checks his bank balance."

"Very sneaky, Mom. I like it."

"Maybe you should think about being sneaky yourself. Calling and texting her only gives her an opportunity to avoid you. It's very difficult to plan for a surprise when you don't know it's coming."

My eyebrows disappear into my hairline. "How did you know?"

She releases a disappointed sigh, one I've heard too many times in my life. "Hunter, we live in a town where everyone knows everyone else. Exactly how many secrets do you think you have from me?"

"Let's change the subject."

"Then let's talk about how long you've been working without a break."

"What are you talking about? I take breaks."

"Sleeping for a few hours at night is not taking time off, son. Twenty-five is way too young to be burned out from working nonstop. You have to get away from here for a while—at least a week or two—to recharge yourself. You've heard of a work-life balance, right? I know you've felt like you had something to prove, but you've achieved that many times over now."

"You know I hate it when you psychoanalyze me."

"No, I haven't even started psychoanalyzing you. I'm simply stating the obvious facts. You're my son, Hunter, and I only want you to be happy."

"I know, Mom, and I appreciate your concern. But I have to do this my way, not your way."

"You are every bit as stubborn as your daddy."

"Must be why you're so crazy over both of us." I wink at her, knowing our stubborn streaks are the spice of her life. Just maybe not the kind of spice she prefers.

"Yes, I'm sure that's the reason why." She rolls her eyes at me playfully. "Hey, do you think you can take Banjo by the vet today? His incision looks a little red to me."

"Sure, Mom. Let me finish a few things around here first, and I'll go by and get him."

With the schedule in hand, I return to the barn to

check the horses and gear before the horde of tourists descends on us later today. My thoughts return to Mallory, as they usually do when I'm alone. I could kick my own ass for pushing her too hard too soon. Especially when I knew better after the way we broke up. But part of me thought if she just remembered the good times, we could get past the bad times faster. Now I realize that was naïve thinking and I've probably lost even more ground with her.

After I've checked and fed all the horses, it's almost time for the next set of tourists to arrive for their horseback ride in the snow. A couple of the wranglers get the horses ready to ride while the guide covers the safety speech. Maybe Mom was right—about everything. A surprise visit to make Mallory talk to me and show her I'm not giving up so easily is in order. And maybe, just maybe, a couple of weeks off work isn't such a bad idea.

All work and no play—all that jazz.

Knowing the customers are in good hands, I head down the mountain and straight to my parents' house. Mom hates taking Banjo to the vet for anything except his shots, but I have a feeling this is a wild goose chase to ease her mind. Maybe my day will get better and Mallory will just happen to be working today. Mal can't blame me for taking good care of the family dog. In no time, I'm walking into the clinic with Banjo in tow, the familiar ringing of the bell over the door as we enter. The young receptionist behind the desk is on the phone, engrossed in a conversation about pet care, so I sign in and take a seat.

When Amelia comes out from the back to call the next pet's name, she scans the full room as she watches to see who stands. Her gaze stops and lingers on me, and I greet her with a smile and a quick wave. She walks over to me and crosses her arms.

"What did you do to her?"

"Nothing. I just wanted to make sure she had a good time."

Amelia raises one eyebrow at me, disbelief written all over her face.

"Fine. Maybe I also wanted to make her miss our old times a little. Is that so bad?"

"Yes. Because any memory of your time together includes your breakup. I suggest starting there if you want to change anything. That is, if she gives you a chance to talk to her again."

"Oh, she'll give me a chance if I have to kidnap her and hold her hostage until she develops Stockholm syndrome." I'm more than determined. This is happening one way or another.

"Good. No excuses, Beckett."

Amelia walks the pet and owner to the back and leaves me with a glimmer of hope. I have Mallory's best friend on my side. That's always a good sign. When it's finally our turn to be seen, Amelia takes us to the exam room and crosses her fingers at me in a sign of good luck before closing the door.

We don't have to wait too long before Mallory opens the door and stops dead in her tracks when she sees me. "Hi." She glances back down at the manila folder in her hand. "You surprised me. I thought Lisa would be here with Banjo. I haven't seen your mom in forever."

"Mom is busy working, but I had a short break, so I brought him for her. She thinks his incision may be getting infected."

"All right, put him up here on the table, and let's see what's going on with his handsome guy."

When he's on the table, she talks to him while petting

him, and he immediately takes to her. Not that I had any doubt—she seems to have that effect on all the Becketts. He relaxes from his rigid stance, and his tail starts wagging fast, like a propeller about to take off in flight. She coaxes him to lie down and scratches his belly, prompting him to roll over without a fight.

Funny, that same trick always worked on me too.

"His incision looks good—maybe just a touch of redness. That's probably from where he has licked it, though. Does he stay inside most of the time?"

"Yes, almost all the time. He's Mom's cure for empty-nest syndrome. She spoils him more than she ever did Dad or me." I laugh and scratch his belly, not admitting that we all pitch in on spoiling the dog.

Mallory looks up at me, her lips parted and eyes wide. When she left for college, I still lived at home. Seems she assumed I still do, but she doesn't appear to want to actually break down and ask me.

"Amelia and I went out riding around the outskirts of town last night so I could show her the rest of the area. We drove by what I now know is your old house. She loved the sleigh ride you arranged the other night, so I was going to show her the barn your family ran them out of a few years ago. But everything was dark and quiet, and I didn't know where you'd moved it."

"Business really picked up, and we needed more space. We added guided horseback rides for the tourists, so we bought the old horse farm at the foot of the mountain and built a bigger barn. Now we have direct access to one of the trails leading up to Santa's Village."

"That was a great idea, Hunter. I bet that was your suggestion."

"Yeah, it was, but one of the trails I use to go up the mountain is the one you and I blazed together."

She looks back down at Banjo and runs her fingers through his coat, slowly nodding her head. "I remember that trail." Her words are spoken so softly, I don't think she meant for me to hear them. "Okay, well, Dad will be with you in just a minute to double-check Banjo, but I don't think his incision is infected."

"You should've been a veterinarian. You're every bit as good at this as your parents are."

"No, I'm really not. I've helped as an assistant with on-the-job training, but I can't be part of euthanizing animals. I bawl my eyes out along with the family—even when it's the best decision for the pet. My sobs don't really help comfort anyone. Anyway, I'd better get to the next patient. Dad will be in here soon." She opens the door and takes a step out of the room.

"Before you go, I want to ask you something."

She looks over her shoulder at me and waits with her eyebrows slightly lifted.

"Did I do something wrong the other night? I thought we were having a good time, but everything seemed to change out of the blue."

"No, you didn't do anything wrong—I had a good time. We're just two old friends who reconnected after a long time apart. Once this semester break is over, I'm going back to Georgia to finish school." She pauses for a moment, her chest rising with the deep breath she draws in. "And after graduation, I don't plan to come back here."

She pulls the door closed behind her as she leaves, taking all the air out of the room with her.

I've known all along there was a possibility she wouldn't come back home after college. After getting a taste of what the world has to offer, she could decide she preferred the fast pace of a big city over the slower lifestyle of small-town living.

But hearing her say the words out loud, confirming what I'd inwardly questioned over the last few years, hurts worse than I thought they could.

"Hello, Hunter. Good to see you again."

I didn't even hear the door open or sense Pete walk into the exam room. I'm still standing in the same spot where Mallory left me, rubbing Banjo to keep him calm. "Hey, Doc. How are you?"

"Good, good. Mallory said she thought the incision looks okay, but let's be sure before we send him back home." Pete's bedside manners are nearly identical to Mal's earlier methods, confirming she watched his every move over the years she grew up in this clinic. "No sign of infection at all. It's normal for the incision to pucker like that as it heals. Tell Lisa not to worry." He describes the signs we should watch for and reminds me to keep Banjo from licking his wound for at least another week or so.

"Thanks, Doc. Mom will be very relieved to hear all is well."

"Hunter?"

I stand after setting Banjo on the floor and meet Pete's gaze. "Yeah?"

"Jackie and I raised Mallory to be independent and self-sufficient. We give her advice when asked and guidance when needed. We try to let her make her own mistakes so she'll learn from the consequences of her decisions, while also shielding her from a lot of the unpleasantness in the world. Maybe we protected her from a little too much, though. There are a few details about the past and the present she doesn't know. Maybe it's time she learns the whole truth."

"What you share with her is up to you, Pete. She makes up her mind without help from anyone else, and she made up her mind about me almost four years ago. You know what I find odd about our split?"

"What's that?"

"She never asked me why. Not once. She never questioned or argued that we belonged together. She never offered a suggestion of how we could make it work while she was in school and I was here working. Before she walked out of this room a few minutes ago, she informed me she's not coming back here after she graduates from college. Her course is set, and I'm not part of it."

"No one's course is set in stone, Hunter. She can change her mind as easily as anyone else can."

"I wouldn't advise holding your breath for that."

CHAPTER NINE

Mallory

"I hate you." I keep my eyes on the road as I drive toward Gran's house. It's officially the last place on God's green earth I want to be.

"You love me, and we both know it." Amelia is unfazed by my bad mood and continues to point out everything she loves about Cringle Cove. "You have no idea how fortunate you are to have grown up somewhere that's almost guaranteed to have a white Christmas. Do you know how many Christmas cartoons, movies, and paintings depict that as the ideal setting? And the people here are so interesting."

"Like who?"

"Like, Chad, for starters."

"You can't use him as an example. You're unusually twitterpated over him. That makes you biased."

"Fine. Hayden Jaxon, then. He's a competitive snowboarder and has endorsement deals. There's Roan McDaniels, the hugely popular country singer, and his brother Grey, who owns The Cove. Even though I haven't met Roan, it's cool that he's from this area. I think I could get used to living in this town and really enjoy it. I may even have a few ideas for bringing in more tourists and sprucing up the Christmas decorations."

"Already putting that marketing degree and your flair for design to use?"

"Always. That's just who I am." She shrugs one shoulder, as if those last five words explain everything.

"You're so funny. Keep kidding around like that, and you'll convince my parents you're considering moving here after college." I laugh out loud at the absurdity of that notion.

"Mal, I'm not kidding. Cringle Cove could really be a great opportunity for my career. It's small, so working with the city council through the tourism department would be easy. They're customer-focused, so they're open to suggestions. This could be a real game changer for me, especially just starting out of college. The more I list the pros and cons, the more pros I find."

"I literally can't believe what I'm hearing, Meli. Is this sudden urge to move to Cringle Cove because of Chad? Are you looking for ways to make a career here work so you can be with a guy you just met?" We roll up to the stop sign, and I openly gawk at her while I wait for her reply.

"No, I'm not that naïve or desperate, and we both know it. I wouldn't hinge my entire career on a man I just met a few days ago and barely know. But getting to know him better could be a perk."

"Wow. Okay. My bad for assuming we'd be roommates for a bit longer after college while we're finding jobs and getting established. But thanks for letting me know now so

I can start making other plans for living arrangements after graduation."

"You could make arrangements to move back to Cringle Cove with me."

"That's not happening. You'll just have to visit me wherever I happen to be living and teaching. You can travel with Mom and Dad when they come to see me."

"Oh, that's yet another perk. I'll be your parents' only daughter when you're not around. By the way, are you going to drive, or are we just going to sit here at the stop sign all morning?"

"Right now, I'm going with sitting here all morning."

We ride the rest of the way to Gran's in mostly silence. Not because I'm sulking over her decision, but because I'm imagining how hard it'll be to say goodbye to her in six months when we graduate. After living with her and seeing her every day for the last four years, I imagine it'll feel a lot like a divorce—one I don't want and didn't initiate, but can't avoid.

What's strange is I've never even considered Amelia wouldn't be part of my everyday life until now. Yes, there are always phone calls, video chats, and the occasional visits, but soon everything I'm used to will completely change. It's a sobering thought, and I'm slightly ashamed that I never considered how my absence has affected my parents. Of course, they want me to live my life and do what makes me happy. But I'm sure they never considered my pursuit of happiness meant they wouldn't be part of my day-to-day life.

It really sucks when the shoe is on the other foot. And that shoe doesn't even fit. Because it's on the opposite foot and makes me walk all wonky.

We pull into Gran's driveway, and I shift the car into

park. Before I reach for the ignition switch, Amelia puts her hand on my arm and stops me.

"You're uncharacteristically quiet. Are you mad at me?"

"No, of course not. I'm just thinking about a lot of things. You know how one thought leads to another, like you start out thinking about the color blue, and you end up in a private bungalow in Bora Bora?"

"Of course. That exact thing happens to everyone." Her deadpan expression makes me smile.

"Anyway. My final conclusion is I'm going to miss you, and now I get a sense of how much my parents have missed me. Especially with my determination to stay away from here because of Hunter and Gran. I've lost so much time with my parents, and for what? The ones I love are the ones who have suffered, and I punished myself for nothing."

"Does that mean you'll move back here with me?"

"No, that's not what I mean. But I will come back and visit you instead of staying away even longer."

"You let me know if you change your mind. I'm sure we can find you a place to stay. A cot or a sleeping bag, maybe."

"You're too kind. Now get your ass out of my car, and go take care of your Gran. You took over my parents, so you have to take her too. She's a package deal." I shrug my shoulders and tilt my head. "I'm sorry for your bad luck."

"Nice try, bestie. You've experienced one major family epiphany today. Let's go in here and see if you have another one." Amelia rarely yields when she has her mind set on something. Like reuniting me with my grandmother.

"It's much more likely that I'll experience a complete break from reality and turn into a screaming banshee."

"In that case, I'll have the camera on my phone set to video. We don't want to miss that opportunity."

Even though I'm still on record as saying this is the worst idea she's ever had, we exit the car and approach the front door. Amelia rings the doorbell, and soon a cheery older lady in nurse's scrubs opens the door.

"Hi. I'm Mallory Conner, and this is my best friend, Amelia Fisher. We're here to see my grandmother, Ernestine."

"Your mom said you were coming. Miss Ernestine is excited to see you. I'm Sue, her caretaker at night. Please come in." She steps aside to give us room to pass. "I'll just grab my coat and be on my way. She's resting in the den, so you two can go on in and see her."

"Thank you, Sue. Drive safe." I walk toward the den with Amelia close behind me. There's nothing quite as awkward as visiting a relative you don't actually want to see.

There she is, resting in her recliner with a thick blanket draped over her. She's lost quite a bit of weight since the last time I saw her. Her cheeks are sunken in, and around her eyes appears hollow, even with them closed. When I thought of her, I always saw the strong, robust woman I'd known all my life. Now, age has caught up with her and is taking its toll. Her recent surgery probably added to the ghostly pallor of her skin, but it can't completely account for her gaunt appearance.

"It's okay to come in, Mallory. I don't have my teeth in, so I can't bite you. And I look worse than I feel. I'm not quite dead yet." She opens one eye and peeks out at us, a small smile playing on her lips. "You're even more beautiful now than when you left for college. You haven't been home in a long time."

"No, I haven't. This is my best friend, Amelia. We go to college together. She's helping out at the clinic while we're on semester break."

"Ah, yes. Amelia. I've heard all about you from Jackie. My son and daughter-in-law are very fond of you."

"The feeling is mutual. I've adopted them as my parents." If Amelia has ever met a stranger in her life, I've never witnessed it. She is as comfortable talking to the college dean as she is with our next-door neighbor. She walks into the room and takes the chair next to Gran, acting as if they're old friends.

The other empty chair must be reserved for me, so I move to the opposite side of the room and take a seat. My discomfort from being back in her house again can't be hidden, though I'm still not sure I even want to try. Why should I pretend everything is okay and let her get away with being such an awful person?

"You know, when Mallory was a little kid, she used to stay with me all the time. If I ran into her on the sidewalk in town, she insisted on coming home with me every time. So I bought a bunch of extra clothes to keep here for her. She called them her special clothes." Gran chuckles weakly, mostly to herself.

"I remember that—I'd forgotten all about it. Seems like that happened during another lifetime now." Nostalgia is a bitch—trying to rob me of the grudge that keeps me warm at night.

"It was during another life. One I'm glad you got out of when you left this town. You'll be happier for it in the long run. I tried to give your father the same advice, but he wouldn't hear it."

Hello, big wooly blanket of resentment, my old friend. I've missed you. For the last forty-five seconds.

"What advice, exactly, did you give Dad?"

"I told him he should move away from here. He deserved to have the entire college experience—moving in to the dorms, having roommates, going to parties, and meeting new people. Life has a funny way of making you appreciate the small things more after you've endured a few hardships. He needed to experience that."

"That's true. Everyone experiences that whether they leave their hometown or not. Whether they go off to college or stay home and work. Whether they follow their mother's advice or not. What makes you think Dad didn't have that same experience? Better yet, what makes you think he needed that experience?

"I've never known him to be unhappy with his life and his choices, and I've known him my whole life. Any moments of sadness he had were caused by you and your actions. I remember the names you called my mother. I remember the cutting remarks you made toward her. The problem was, I didn't understand any of it when I was a kid. But I'm not a kid anymore."

The shocked expression on her face is priceless. Even when my parents were quarreling with her, I never heard either of them put her in her place. They tried their best to keep the peace and not stoop to her level, but I'm not as nice as my parents are.

"You're right, Mallory. I was wrong for pushing what I wanted on him the way I did. At the time, I thought I was doing what was best for him. You'll find out one day when you have kids of your own. They don't come with an instruction manual. What works perfectly for one could end in disaster with another. When I graduated from high school, I didn't have the option of going off to college. It was completely out of reach for me, but I wanted to give my son the best. Only, he already had the best—because he had Jackie and you."

"When did you come to this conclusion?"

"I suppose I've known it all along, but I was forced to accept it recently. Now that I've gotten past my own ego, I can see where I was wrong in how I handled it."

"Well, thank God for small miracles, right?"

Gran cuts her eyes at me, narrowing them as she stares at me. Amelia clears her throat before she interrupts the full conversation occurring in silence.

"So, Gran. Have you watched *Game of Thrones* yet? If not, I suggest we have a marathon today to catch you up, complete with junk food and Jell-O shots."

"Amelia, I like the way you think, little girl. You have yourself a date."

Her plan works like a charm. We old-lady-sit Gran for the rest of the day and into the evening until her nightly caregiver returns. All the insults I wanted to hurl at her evaporate when I'm sucked into the fictional world of my favorite show. We make sure she's well fed and help her every time she stands.

But nothing is resolved.

Something tells me we'll revisit the huge elephant in the middle of the room. We've danced around him long enough.

On the way back home, Amelia, being Amelia, states the obvious.

"Hunter didn't call or text you at all today." She tries to sound so nonchalant, but she fails.

"Nope."

"I think it bothers you even more than you're showing."

"I'm not showing anything. What are you talking about?"

"Do I really have to spell everything out for you? All right then, you asked for it. You are crazy for turning away a good man who is obviously trying to win you back. Especially when you're still in love with him. You're just scared. You've turned into an overgrown scaredy-cat, and you need to snap out of it because you're embarrassing me."

"Let me know when you're ready to tell me what you really think instead of holding back. We'll talk then."

There's her smartass snicker again.

CHAPTER TEN

Hunter

When my phone rings, I stare at the screen in disbelief. The name that flashes up shocks the shit out of me, rendering me mute for a moment.

Something must be wrong.

"Hello?"

"Hey, Hunter. This is Mallory. Are you busy?"

"Not too bad right now. What's on your mind?"

"You went to a lot of trouble to plan and coordinate everything for us the other night, and I realized I acted like a total bitch. I want to apologize for not being more appreciative. And I wanted to ask if you're free to maybe hang out together tomorrow. I know it's short notice, but I hoped your schedule would slow down some since it's only a couple of days until Christmas."

I'm stunned speechless from her apology and her request. She willingly wants to spend the day with me? Is this a Hallmark movie in disguise?

"Hunter? Did I lose you?"

Never.

"No, I'm here. Just surprised, honestly. First of all, you don't owe me an apology for anything. I sprang that night on you out of left field. But I appreciate the gesture. As far as spending the day together tomorrow, I think I can make that happen. How about I pick you up at nine in the morning? I have the perfect idea."

"That sounds great. How should I dress?"

"Comfortable and warm. Wear your good boots."

"I know you don't mean my Chanel boots by that comment."

"Not in the least."

"Okay. I'll see you tomorrow morning, then. I'm looking forward to it, Hunter. And thank you for being so amiable about all of this."

"My pleasure, Snagglepuss. We'll have fun and enjoy the day."

After we disconnect, I stand rooted to my spot for a few more minutes, just smiling like a crazy man.

"Are you and that horse eloping, or are you ready to move on to the next one?" Chad deadpans as he passes by the stall.

Have I mentioned how great working with my best friend is?

"Definitely eloping. We've already picked out our honeymoon spot."

After I finish working in the barn, I head to the office to find Mom. She's busy in front of the computer screen again, but this time with a huge grin on her face.

"Are you watching porn at work again, Mom?" Her face turns bright red, and I bust out laughing at her expense. Again. After the first hundred times, you'd think she'd get used to my teasing.

"No, I'm not. Your dad and I wait to watch that together."

"Whoa—good one, Mom! I didn't expect that comeback. I'm impressed. What are you grinning about, then?"

"I just finished pulling almost all the financials for the end of the year—well, considering there's only about a week left this year, it's basically all. And this has been the most profitable year ever. I'm just so proud of you and what you've accomplished with this business."

It's never been about the money for me, though it is a nice benefit.

"Glad to hear it, Mom. And you'll be glad to hear what I'm about to tell you."

"Oh? Does it involve grandchildren anytime soon?"

"No. But I am taking the day off tomorrow, so that's a step in the right direction."

"You're taking off work? The whole day?" She looks at me with one eyebrow slightly raised, waiting for the punch line.

"That's right. The whole day."

"Why? Are you sick? Do you need to go to the hospital?" She sits back and crosses her arms.

"No, I'm fine, and you know it. I'm spending the day with Mallory tomorrow…and this was even her idea."

"That's exciting news. I'm happy for you, son. And I'm very glad you're actually taking a day off. I'll make sure your work is covered by someone else right this minute. In fact, you should go ahead and leave now."

"You know what? You're right. Everything here is covered for the rest of the evening. I'm heading home early."

"Have fun tomorrow."

AT NINE ON THE DOT, I RING THE DOORBELL AT Mallory's, more excited than a little kid on Christmas morning. She tried to keep the conversation casual when she called yesterday, not admitting our time together means almost as much to her as it does to me. But I heard it in her voice—the hesitancy mixed with the hopefulness.

Or maybe that was the sound of my voice.

Either way, I'm just a guy, standing here in front of a closed door, hoping the girl I let go finds her way back to me. Preferably before I'm forced to resort to clubbing her over the head and dragging her off to my cave until she comes to her senses. If not, four or five years as my cave guest should do it.

The door opens, and the most beautiful girl in the world smiles up at me. She sticks her right leg out to show off her boots. "Are these good enough? They're both comfy and warm."

"Those are perfect. Are you ready to head out now?"

She picks up a small bag from the foyer table, pulls the strap over her head, and drapes it across her body. "I am now."

After she locks the door behind her, she starts walking toward my truck. "Are you not going to tell anyone you're leaving?"

"They're already gone. Mom is at Gran's again. Amelia went in to work with Dad, but they didn't need me. Dad is only seeing patients half a day today, and they're discharging the animals that had surgery recently during the last part of the day."

"So no one would notice if I just decided to kidnap you and keep you all to myself?"

She stops walking and looks over her shoulder at me with a sly smile on her face and in her eyes. "Oh, they'd notice, all right. And they'd probably pay you to keep me."

"That sounds like a win-win to me. Getting paid for keeping you all to myself and making you my personal love slave? I'll take that combination any day."

"You'll get tired of me and want to get rid of me in no time. Trust me."

After we climb into the truck, I wait to start the engine until she looks over at me. "I've known you most of your life, Mallory. I haven't gotten tired of you yet. I think it's safe to say I never will."

Her face falls a little before she catches herself. "Let's just try getting through one day first and see how you do with that."

A simple nod is my only reply before starting the truck and our day together. The sidewalks in town are full of people doing last-minute shopping, picking up a few more stocking stuffers and extra food before the big day arrives. "Have you finished your Christmas shopping?"

Small talk always helps break the ice. Right?

"Actually, I finished earlier than normal this year. I'm usually one of these people, picking through whatever's left over because I couldn't make my mind up earlier in the season. Have you?"

"Yep—no shopping for us today. I have other plans."

"What do your plans include? You didn't give me any clues other than comfy and warm boots."

"That's all the clues you need right now. You'll see soon enough."

Our idle chat carries on until we nearly reach our destination. That's when she suddenly stops talking and takes notice of where we are—and where we're headed. I turn into my driveway and flaunt my sly smile in her direction. "Thought we'd have some fun away from the crowds today."

"Sounds good to me. I've dealt with enough people in the clinic this week to last a lifetime. The whole town brought their pets in before the holidays hit."

"A day with no social interaction is just what the veterinarian ordered, then. Let's have some fun."

Her eyes are fixed on our surroundings when I slip out of the truck and walk around to open her door. With her hand in mine, I help her out and lace our fingers together, keeping the connection intact while we walk toward the barn.

"Hunter, this place is beautiful. The old horse farm I remember was barely kept up. You must've worked day and night on everything—the fence, the barn, and even the driveway." She turns to look around, still holding on to my hand, before looking at me. "This really is an amazing place now. I'm so proud of you."

"Come on. Let me show you around."

We walk through the barn first. The outside is large but unpretentious, not giving away the secrets held inside. The long, wide corridor is lined with offices and stalls. The entire inside is tongue-in-groove wood slats, stained in a rich English Walnut shade. When I first started my business, I considered doing everything out of one barn. Having loads of strangers at my place on a daily basis quickly changed my mind about that idea.

Today, I'm infinitely thankful for our privacy. The constant hustle and bustle of a busy working barn doesn't exactly create a romantic atmosphere for rekindling old flames. But our seclusion today gives Mallory a chance to remember every little thing about us. Like how we spent so much time on horseback, scoping out the mountain trails and looking for places to blaze new ones. The horses hear us and poke their heads out, looking for food and attention. Good thing Mallory is willing to provide that to them in spades.

"Is my favorite horse here?" She lovingly strokes the first one she rushed to, grabbing a handful of grain on her way to hand-feed him.

Her horse is a black Tennessee Walker named Jet. He was the one she rode every time we went out on the trail. Every weekend, we rode the same path and cut the trail that leads off this property now and up to Santa's Village.

"He sure is, and he's waiting for you."

Her head jerks up, and her jaw drops open. "Where?"

She quickly scans the other half-doors until she sees his head emerge from inside the stall. She moves swiftly to greet him, slowing only enough not to scare him with her sudden movements. With a soft voice, she speaks to him, calling him by his name until she's sure he remembers her. She reaches up to rub him behind his ear, and he lowers his head until his jaw rests on her shoulder.

Just like old times.

Her other arm moves up to his neck until they're embraced in a full hug. Jet knows her, without a doubt, and is just as happy to be with her again as she is to see him. I step behind her and rub his muzzle as I say hello.

"Hey, Jet. Looks like your girl is home. You've missed her, haven't you, buddy? You look happy to have her back again."

"He didn't miss me. He didn't even know I was gone."

"The hell he didn't. He looked for you every time he

saw me. He'd run the fence line, neighing loudly, calling for you. He finally gave up after a while of not finding you."

"I'm sorry I left you, Jet. I've missed you too, buddy. More than I even realized." She turns her face toward me, and I see tears glistening in her eyes. "You don't fight fair."

"No such thing as a fair fight, babe. And when the stakes are this high, I'll do whatever I have to do to win."

"To win what?"

"You, of course. Everything I do is for you. Always has been. Always will be."

"Hunter, you make it damn near impossible to stay mad at you."

"Good. I'm glad to hear that. Now, are you ready to saddle him up and go for a ride in the snow?"

"Absolutely. I'm ready to go right now."

She leads Jet out of his stall and finds his gear in the tack room. I watch her as I get my horse ready. She takes her time grooming him first, talking to him, and stroking his thick winter coat with her fingers. When we're finished with the last pieces, I help her up onto his back before we ride toward the trail.

They move as one unit, their movements synchronized and fluid. Her broad smile says more than her words could convey. She's truly happy for the first time since she's been home. The reason why she lost that spark is all my fault. If only I'd found another way out of our predicament. But no good comes from dwelling on what went wrong in the past. All I can do is rectify those mistakes in the present.

"He's just as smooth as I remember. Who's been riding my horse to keep him in shape?" The challenge in her tone makes me smile.

"Mostly me. Chad rides him too. Sometimes, the other

trail guides will take him out for a spin. He's not really a beginner's horse, so none of the guests ride him."

"Good. I don't like other people riding my horse."

"Fine by me. As long as you come back and ride him yourself every week." She doesn't agree, but then, she doesn't disagree either. I'm counting that as progress.

Halfway up the trail, we stop to give the horses a break while we explore on foot. She stops a few paces ahead of me and stoops down to examine something on the ground.

"What'd you find?"

Before I know what hits me, she's cackling and running to hide behind a tree. I dry off my face from the snowball she just pegged me with, then scoop up a handful of my own. Another one zings past my face before I find shelter, and her laughter carries on the mountain breeze all around me. It's the sweetest sound I've heard in forever. Or, technically, the past several years.

We exchange trash talk as the snowballs hurtle past, sometimes connecting but mostly just barely missing the target. We move through the trees stealthily, using them as shields and hiding spots as we try to get closer to the other. Never mind that her constant giggling gives away her position—it's the thrill of the chase that we're enjoying the most.

While she's busy making an arsenal, I steal up behind her and wait for her to realize I'm there. When she finally senses me standing close to her, she shrieks loudly then laughs even harder. She tries to stand to run away, but her hands are full of snowballs she doesn't want to crush, so she stumbles a few steps. I use her imbalance to my advantage and tackle her to the ground, caging her in my arms to soften the landing.

One minute, we're laughing and play-fighting, trying to

smear snow in each other's faces and shove handfuls into each other's shirts. The next minute, our lips are locked in a heated kiss and the rest of the world has ceased to exist. Her gloved hands slide across my scalp. Her fingers grip my hair, tugging lightly when our kiss deepens. Every taste of her drives me to need more—like a constant craving flowing through my veins. The velvety feel of her tongue gliding against mine is its own aphrodisiac, never quite giving me enough to quench my thirst.

It's strange how a kiss answers a million questions with only one word. Mallory. She's everything I need. All that I want. And the only woman I love—have ever loved and will ever love. Without a doubt, I will never be completely happy or feel whole without her by my side. I've always known no one else could take her place in my life and my heart. This kiss simply seals my fate—it's her or no one for me.

Somewhere in the back of my mind, a realization that she's still lying on her back in the snow brings me out of my Mallory-induced oblivion long enough to break the kiss. When I pull away and look into her eyes, I see my own emotions mirrored in her gaze. Knowing my Mallory, she'll fight this feeling when she comes to her senses. She'll try to put us back in a little box, pushing it into the back of her mind. Out of sight, out of mind.

What I need is a plan to ensure she doesn't run away from me again.

CHAPTER ELEVEN

Mallory

My toes are still tingling after that kiss.

Hunter helps me back up on Jet, and we ride the rest of the way up the mountain. When we reach the sleigh trail from the other night, I realize exactly where we are. "Oh my God, Hunter! You didn't tell me our old trail leads to Santa's Village. Do you use this trail for your guided rides too?"

"Not exactly. It does join with it just down the trail a little way, though."

When we reach the barn at the end of the trail, we get off and lead the horses inside. After we take the saddles off and put the horses in their stalls, we walk toward Santa's Workshop to get a cup of hot coffee. When Hunter doesn't reach for my hand right away, I sense something missing—as if it's a part of me. So I reach over and take his hand first, and that sense of wholeness I crave is instantly fulfilled.

He looks down at our hands then meets my stare, not

even trying to hide his sexy little smirk. "Don't think I'll put out just because I kissed you. I mean, it was a great kiss. But you'll have to work a little harder if you want in my pants."

At first, I'm so shocked by his sarcastic jab I can't even think of a good comeback line. I openly gawk at him—and I mean a wide-open gawk. My eyes refuse to blink. My mouth refuses to shut. My brain can't think of a single witty retort. Then the hilarity of it hits me all at once, and I bend at the waist in a fit of laughter. My arm goes to my stomach, holding it as I laugh, the muscles tightening with each outburst.

After a minute, I can't catch my breath and can envision myself in an episode of *That '70s Show*, when they're in the basement laughing uncontrollably as they pass the joint around. Tears roll down my cheek and I try to wipe them away, but they're quickly replaced by more. When I look up at Hunter, the most amused expression covers his face—along with a little bit of embarrassment because now everyone is looking at us. That combination only makes me laugh harder. When I finally bring myself back under control, I wipe the final tears away and grin up at him. "That was the funniest shit I've heard in a long time."

"I'm glad you find my virtue so amusing."

"Oh, it's not your virtue I find funny, Santa. It's that you said you wouldn't put out like you really meant it. Maybe you forgot, but I already know better than to think you're innocent. You're the one who taught me how to be naughty." I giggle to myself as we continue walking hand in hand.

He stops me with a quick jerk of my hand, making me simultaneously turn toward him and stumble into his hard chest. His other arm wraps around my waist, pulling me firmly against him. Those chocolate-brown-with-flecks-of-gold eyes bore into mine, and I feel him touching me all the way down to my soul. "Trust me, babe. That is one thing I'll never forget. Don't tell anyone or you'll ruin my good reputation, but you just say the word, and we'll check off every item on that Naughty List tonight."

It's suddenly scorching hot in Santa's Village…and the outside temperature has nothing to do with the heat level. I'm a little weak in the knees too. Butterflies flutter in my stomach. My heart races. My mouth is dry. My chest heaves with each deep breath.

I really want to say yes. Right now.

"If you don't quit looking at me like that, Chief Land will arrest us both any second now. We'll be in the *Cringle Cove Busted* paper—with side-by-side mug shots."

"Give me a second. Right now, I'm thinking it'll be worth it. I'm waiting to see if my brain starts working again, though."

"There's my Mallory. Welcome back." He releases his hold on me and takes a step backward, putting some space between us before we embarrass ourselves.

"Coffee?" Change the subject. Change the subject. Change the subject.

"Come on, you little jezebel. I'll buy you a white chocolate mocha and the biggest cinnamon roll they have."

"You had me at jezebel."

His rich, manly chuckle carries on the chilly air, and he releases my hand, wrapping his arm around me instead. This all feels like old times…like we've never been apart… like we were always supposed to be together.

But if that were true, we wouldn't have broken up nearly four years ago. If he can make me feel so loved, so cherished within a few hours of spending time together, why did I feel so unlovable when he broke my heart?

What's wrong with me?

"You're overthinking it." He glances over at me, no hint of a smile or playfulness.

"What did you say?"

"I said, you're overthinking it. Again. Like you always do. Just chill out. Let everything happen the way it's supposed to, and don't try to overanalyze every minute detail in that gorgeous brain of yours."

Don't overthink it. Don't analyze it. Just let it happen. Does that mean we're just a fling now? Maybe a romp in the sheets for old times' sake before we go our separate ways again?

"Mallory, there's smoke coming out of your ears from the gears turning so fast. Slow it down. Let's enjoy our drinks and our company, then we'll decide the next thing on our to-do list for the day."

"All right. I am officially relaxing now."

"It's good that you made a declaration about relaxing. Really sets the chilled mood I was going for."

"I'm glad I could help. We're chilled, and now it's time to warm up. Go get my coffee and cinnamon roll you promised me." I slide into the seat of an empty table and wait for Hunter to return with my goodies. My phone buzzes in my pocket, and I know there's only one person it can be.

Amelia: *How's your all-day date going?*

Me: *Fine.*

Amelia: *One-word answers are inappropriate in this case. Details. Now.*

Me: *Rode horses. Kissed. Had a moment of*

rekindled fire. Flames quickly extinguished by reality.

Amelia: *Stop looking for what's wrong with him and enjoy everything that's right.*

Me: *Shut up.*

I can hear her laughing all the way up here on the mountain.

The thing is, I know she's right. She knows she's right. But I don't really want to admit this to her out loud. I do always look for something wrong so I can get rid of the guy as fast as possible. It's not like I've found something petty wrong with Hunter. No toenail fungus. No finger-like toes. No annoying habits after we kiss. Outwardly, he's great—as close to perfect as I've ever found. Inwardly, I always used to think he was the best guy I knew, apart from my dad, of course.

When I boil it all down to a single issue, the problem becomes much easier to digest. It's trust…or a lack of trust, to be more precise. I can't trust him with my heart anymore. So, I can't give it to him again.

With that settled in my mind, now I can relax and have fun. If I don't let him in my head and my heart, leaving Cringle Cove at the end of our break will be easier than it was the first time. I won't be nursing a heart that's been smashed into a million pieces this time.

Hunter approaches the table with two large mugs and two plates with enormous cinnamon rolls on them. The steam from the mugs and the warmed plates mix, setting off the sweet aroma and making me practically drool in anticipation.

"Mmm, that smells so good." I stand to help unload the treats from his hands. We dig in with our fingers, ignoring the strange looks from the people around us when we smack our lips in appreciation. "I guess it's a good thing I don't live here. I'd be as big as a barn with these available year-round."

"Nah. We'd keep it worked off of you one way or another." He waggles his eyebrows at me while opening his eyes as wide as possible. That goofy move always makes me laugh. "By the way, we have a small change in plans. Chad called a few minutes ago. He said one of the horses on today's ride threw a shoe, so they need to use my horse for the trip back down the mountain. We'll drive his car today, and tomorrow I can ride Jet back down the trail to my barn."

"Sounds like you've got it all worked out. But, for the record, if you're trying to get rid of me early, you don't have to make up such an elaborate story. Just take me home, and we're good."

"I'm not trying to get rid of you early, and you're not getting out of spending the day with me. A deal's a deal, Mal."

"I'm just saying." I shrug my shoulders casually, conveying I'm fine either way. I'm not, but I'll make sure he believes it no matter what.

"So am I." He looks at me pointedly, and his point is taken.

"Fine. Have it your way. What's next on the agenda?"

"TELL ME THE REST! WHAT ELSE DID YOU TWO DO yesterday?" Have I mentioned Amelia is very demanding?

"Where was I? Oh yes, the horse threw a shoe. Then we took Chad's car and parked on Main Street. We walked up and down the street, window-shopping like tourists. We stopped and listened to the choir singing Christmas carols in the church. We ate junk food all day. Then we went to the Christmas play and drove around the lake to look at all the Christmas lights and decorations on those houses."

"You make it all sound so exciting. I'm thrilled to death listening to you go blah, blah, blah. Could you be more boring right now?"

"Fine. You want to hear the juicy stuff? Then let me get right to the point."

"Finally! It's about damn time. Tell me!"

"After the play and the drive, he took me back to his house. I never saw it when we were at his barn yesterday morning. Meli, it is absolutely stunning. He built an enormous log cabin up against the mountain. It sits behind a grove of white pines, so it's completely secluded from the rest of the world. It has a huge front porch. The kitchen is to die for—and oh my God, the bathrooms!

"I don't know how many acres he has, but it's a lot. I sat on the front porch swing, bundled up in a blanket and drinking hot chocolate, just watching the snow fall. I'd forgotten how beautiful the snow can be. I know that's because I never see it anymore, but his place could be in a Norman Rockwell painting."

"This whole town could be, Mal. It's gorgeous here. And you miss it more than you'll admit. You miss Hunter a lot. Like, a lot, a lot. You only wish you didn't."

"What if you're right? It wouldn't change anything. We can't change the past, and the future is already mapped out. My life plans don't involve moving back here after graduation."

"I ran into the principal for the elementary school last night."

"How do you know you met the principal?"

"Chad introduced me to her. She's very nice."

"Good for you and Chad."

"We started talking, and I mentioned you were graduating with a degree in early childhood education in less than six months. She was very interested in talking to you about a position. One of her teachers is having a baby just before the end of the school year and doesn't plan to return after maternity leave. How many of our classmates can say they have a job waiting for them as soon as they graduate?"

"You know how much I hate it when you are all logical and sensical."

"Well, you are welcome to stew on it all day while I'm off with Chad. I'm not crashing his family's Christmas Day festivities when I just met him this week, but I will totally hijack him Christmas Eve for our own festivities. Later, Mal."

"Later, hussy. Have fun with Chad." I wink, letting her know I'm joking.

"Oh, don't even go there." She waves goodbye and walks out the door with such a spring in her step, I'd swear she bounced.

Dad walks into the den and sits down across from me. He picks up the newspaper and starts reading it. I swear, I think he's the only person I know who still gets the newspaper delivered to his home instead of just reading the news online.

"You've been spending a lot of time with Hunter lately. Something going on there I need to know about?"

"Not really. We're just old friends catching up on everything that's new in our lives. That's about it."

"If you say so."

Before I can retort, Dad's phone rings with the distinctive tone alerting him to an emergency call. He picks it up before the first ring even finishes.

"Dr. Conner. Yes. How's his breathing? How long ago did this happen? Can you move him? Okay, meet me at the office as soon as you can. I'll be waiting there for you."

He jumps up and grabs his jacket from the coatrack. "Mallory, I need you to come with me. Call your mom on the way and tell her to meet us at the clinic. I'll probably need her help with surgery. A friend's dog was hit by a car a few minutes ago. From what they said, he's not in good shape."

I grab my coat and rush out to the car with Dad, fumbling with my phone to reach Mom. This is why I can't do what they do. If I lost that dog, I'd be an emotional wreck for days. They understand they can't save every animal—they do the best they can with what they have to work with. But I'm not made like that. Adrenaline doesn't make me work better—it makes me drop my phone and dial wrong numbers.

"Mom!" I finally reach her and relay the message from Dad while he drives, weaving around one car after the other on our little two-lane road in our two-red-light town.

We rush inside, not knowing how soon they'll be here with the injured dog. Dad changes clothes for surgery, and I turn on all the lights, sterilize my hands, and make sure all the instruments they'll need are ready. Dad joins me in the surgery area and helps finish the last of the preparations before we hear the bell over the front door.

"Dr. Conner?" a frantic voice calls down the hall, so I rush out to help him as much as I can. An older man is carrying a large chocolate lab wrapped up in a blanket. The man's eyes are red-rimmed and his face is splotchy.

"Dad's in the back getting ready for you. What's your dog's name?"

"Bear."

"Go ahead and bring Bear back here. We'll take good care of him."

Dad steps out from the surgery room. "Right here, Sam. Let's put him on the table then we can take a good look at him."

A few seconds pass before I hear the jingle of the front door opening. "Mallory? Pete?"

"Back here, Mom."

She goes through the same sterilization procedures as Dad then joins him in the surgery room. Dad is taking X-rays, and I know what comes next—prepping Bear for surgery. I really don't want to be around for that, but I won't leave them to handle the worst part alone. Add to that, Bear's dad is really distraught, so I couldn't leave him alone even if I wanted.

"Sam, he needs surgery right now." Dad goes into the explanation of an internal bleed that needs to be stopped right away and a broken leg that needs to be set and secured with screws.

Sam just nods his head, barely able to speak. "Do what you have to. Please just save him."

Right there—that's all it took for tears to spring to my eyes.

"Come with me, Sam. Let's go wait out front together so Mom and Dad can work on Bear without us interrupting them."

"Okay. My wife will be here in a minute. She had to take the grandkids home. They were pretty upset too."

"We'll wait for her together." I wrap my hand around his elbow and walk with him down the long corridor. I know a little of how he feels—I want Bear to be okay too. Soon his wife joins us, and they talk quietly among themselves about how the grandkids are doing after the trauma, how Bear got away from them while chasing his ball, and how they wish they could go back in time and just change that one thing. That one awful moment.

I can relate.

CHAPTER TWELVE

Hunter

"Hunter, I hate to bother you today, but I think you'd better come up here. One of the sleigh horses seems colicky. I don't think we can wait too much longer to treat him."

It's Christmas Eve. And I'd planned on spending the evening with Mallory, although I haven't told her yet. I wanted to surprise her with a quiet, romantic, candlelit dinner at my place. Maybe a stroll in the snow. Definitely pick up where we left off the other night.

Instead, I'll probably get to spend tonight in a barn, caring for my horse and making sure he's better by morning.

"You're right—we really can't wait if it's truly colic. I'm leaving right now, so give me about fifteen minutes." I hang up with the wrangler on duty and throw on my coat. I'm probably facing a very long night.

Before leaving, I pour the entire carafe of coffee into an extra-large thermos and grab a few snacks from the pantry just in case the cupboards are bare in the barn office. When I step outside, the frigid air cuts right through me, as expected for this time of year, but the slivers of ice in the air are new.

And unwelcome.

I double-time it up the mountain, my lead foot serving its purpose today as I race to the barn. If that 2000-pound draft horse does have colic, it could mean life or death for him. And it means he's in a lot of pain right now. Time is of the essence, and I'd rather be safe than sorry when it comes to my animals.

With the number of horses and pets my family has, the local vet's office is on my list of favorites in my phone. After a few rings, Pete picks up the phone—surprising me since it's Christmas Eve and I thought I'd have to go through the answering service to get him on the line.

"Hey Doc, it's Hunter. Listen, I'm sorry to bother you today, and you must already have an emergency case there if you're in the office, but I may need your help up at Santa's Village." I relay the information my wrangler gave me and practically beg him to meet me as soon as possible.

"Hunter, you know I'm more than willing to help you, but we have our hands full here right now. Jackie is still in the operating room with Bear. He was hit by a car, and everything is touch and go at the moment. I actually just stepped out to give Sam an update and knew this call must be another emergency.

"Mallory is here with me and helped until Jackie could get here from my mother's. Mallory has watched Jackie and me work with animals all her life, and she definitely knows horses. She'll know if this case is more than she can safely treat. If you trust us, I can send Mallory up there right now with all the essentials."

"Yes, absolutely. I trust both of you, and I'd be very grateful if she can meet me and help. Thank you so much, Pete."

"No need to thank me, Hunter. Mallory will be there as soon as she can, and I will call and check in on your horse when we get Bear stabilized."

We disconnect, and even though I'm still very concerned about my horse, the heaviness in my chest is relieved somewhat knowing Mallory will be with me. Pete was right about her—she has watched her parents work their magic with sick animals all her life. All I can do now is hope we're not too late to save him. The nearest horse surgery center isn't close to our little town at all, and I'm positive they're closed for the holidays.

My truck comes to a sliding halt outside the barn, and I rush inside to assess the situation myself. When I reach Blue's stall, I find him pawing the ground and biting at his side. His food remains untouched, all obvious signs the big guy is in pain. He sighs and shifts on his feet at the same time, telling me he doesn't feel good at all in the only way he can. I step inside the stall and slip the rope halter over his head before connecting the lead rope.

"Come on, Blue. Let's go for a walk and see if that helps at all."

"That probably won't help him." Mallory approaches from behind me with a duffel bag full of supplies. I'm instantly grateful she came overly prepared for the task. "Walking a horse with a mild case of colic may temporarily distract him, but it mainly just makes the owner feel better by thinking they're doing something more than simply watching their animal in pain."

"I still say you should've been a vet, Mal. By all means, tell me what we need to do to help him, then."

She takes the lead rope from my hand and walks him back into the stall. "You're a big, handsome guy, aren't you? I'll take care of you—don't worry."

She speaks to him in a calm, soothing voice, scratching his neck and giving him time to acclimate to her presence before she starts poking and prodding him. She's a natural with animals, especially horses. She understands them, and they sense her comfort with them in turn. He's still in pain, but he lowers his head and licks his lips a few times, signaling his submission.

She pulls the stethoscope out first and presses it against his side. Her brows draw down, and she stands stock-still, listening intently and not speaking. I want to ask a hundred and one questions, but I bite my tongue instead. When she's finished with that, she finds the thermometer in the bag and takes his temperature next. Then she checks his mouth, looking on the top and bottom all around. Next, she moves to his left side and runs her finger along his bottom jaw then stops and looks at her watch for several seconds.

"Good boy. Now it's time for the not so fun part, big guy."

"Can you tell me what you're doing first? You're killing me here."

"Sure. I listened for bowel sounds, and I still hear them, so that is a positive sign. Then I took his temperature —it is slightly elevated, but not in the danger zone. Then I checked his gums. They're still a healthy pink all around. I just finished taking his pulse, which is fast because of the pain. Now, I have to examine him to hopefully tell what type of colic we're dealing with without having to wait for Dad to come up here. I think I know what it is, but I need to be sure."

"How do you do that?"

She reaches into the bag and pulls out a plastic glove… one that's long enough to reach all the way up to her shoulder.

"Oh."

"I'm going to insert a gastric tube first through his nostril. Mom and Dad taught me how to do it years ago in case my horse ever developed colic and I had to react in an emergency situation. I'm ninety-nine percent sure we're dealing with an impaction, but this will help tell us for sure. Hold his head while I guide the tube in—I have to be able to feel where the tube goes to make sure it's in the correct passage."

The twelve-foot-long tube slowly disappears into Blue's nose while Mallory watches his every reaction with extra attention. She occasionally speaks softly to him, repeating "good boy" over and over. Those are words he's familiar with, and he understands he's doing exactly what she's asking him to do. When she finally stops feeding the tube in, I hear a rush of gas through the tube and immediately detect the sweet smell of grass.

"Is that a good sign?"

"Yes, it is. He doesn't have any fluid built up in his stomach, so that's a very good sign. Now for the intestinal exam."

She sticks her hand into the ginormous glove and pulls the end up to her shoulder. Then she removes the outer sterile plastic covering, revealing the lubricant covering the latex glove. She moves behind Blue, running her ungloved hand along his body to tell him where she's standing at all times. I watch with a mixture of profound gratitude and morbid curiosity as she performs the exam without hesitation.

"You're such a good boy, Blue. We'll make you feel better in just a minute, buddy." She disposes of the glove and walks out of the stall. "Stay there with him. I need to wash my hands and call Dad to give him an update. I'll be right back."

Within a couple of minutes, she returns with her phone held out, relaying all the vital signs to Pete and explaining all the steps she's taken so far. "He's in pain, so I'm thinking I need to give him pain medicine to make this more tolerable for him. The nasogastric tube is in place, so we can easily administer the laxatives. I just need to know how much pain meds to give him. He's huge, Dad."

She turns the face of the phone toward Blue so Pete can see what she's done. She goes through the basic steps again—showing his gums, taking his pulse, and listening again for bowel sounds. When Pete is reassured of her diagnosis, he relays the correct dosage and watches as Mallory administers it. When Blue's head droops and his lips hang loose, we know the medication is working and he's feeling no pain.

"That's another good sign. If the medicine didn't stop the pain, we'd be looking at a more severe case." Pete continues to give the dosage for the laxatives and instructions for getting more fluids into Blue now that we know the problem isn't currently life-threatening. He watches over video chat as she pushes the medicine through the tube, directly into Blue's stomach. "Now you just need to watch him closely—and I mean check on him every fifteen or twenty minutes. This type of colic rarely requires surgery, but we can't take any chances. Every horse is different, and so is every case of colic."

"We'll keep an eye on him and let you know if anything at all changes. Thanks, Dad. Love you."

"Love you, Mal. You did a great job with him, honey. Your mom and I are proud of you."

Mallory blows her dad a kiss before disconnecting. She pockets her phone and turns to me. "Looks like we're spending Christmas Eve right here in this stall. I hope you didn't have big family plans tonight."

"I definitely had plans in mind for tonight, but not with my family. Actually, I wanted to spend it with you, so I guess I got my wish. Just not in the way I imagined. Wait right here, and I'll grab us a couple of comfortable chairs to relax in since we're stuck in here for a while. That is, unless you need to leave?"

"No, I wouldn't leave you alone with this. You hide it well, but I can tell you're still really worried about him. I'm staying. At least until we know he's out of the woods."

"Thank you, Mallory. That means more to me than you know. I'll be right back."

"Take your time. Blue and I aren't going anywhere."

Walking at a brisk pace, I head to the kitchen and rummage through the refrigerator and cabinets before throwing together a dinner for two. With the inside cameras on, I put Blue's stall front and center on the large monitor then grab a couple of warm blankets from the closet. Mallory's time home from Georgia is about to come to an end, so this is my now-or-never moment. If she leaves without admitting her feelings for me, without admitting she misses us, I'll never get another chance to win her back.

When the food is ready, I walk back down the hall and stick my head in the stall. "Hey, while he's still sedated, why don't we have a bite to eat out on the deck? I'll turn on the patio heaters, light the fire pit, and we can cover up with the blankets. We can watch Blue on the monitor, and you can check his vitals again after we eat."

"Sounds good—I'm starving. Let me check them again right now before I leave him, though." She goes through all the motions again, documenting the numbers as she goes, then washes up on her way out.

When we open the door leading outside, we both halt in our tracks, and Mallory gasps audibly. It's completely dark outside now, meaning we've been inside longer than I realized. But the scene in front of us is unbelievable. Huge, fluffy snowflakes are falling, adding to the inch of snow that already covers the ground and the deck. They don't immediately melt when they land on my skin, and they aren't melting at all when they hit the ground. From the looks of the clouds overhead, I don't think it'll stop snowing anytime soon.

The large round patio daybed is mostly shielded by its sloping canopy, providing the perfect shelter in which to relax and watch the snowflakes sparkle in the firelight. I motion toward the comfortable cushions. "Have a seat, and I'll get the heaters and fire pit going."

"You know, I'd forgotten how beautiful snowfall can be. I know it's a pain in the ass after so many days in a row. But it's nice when you've been away for a while." She brushes the snow off the edge of the outdoor daybed before making herself comfortable under the covering. "This is perfect."

"I'm not sure how perfect our Christmas Eve dinner will be. We don't have a lot of food here that can be cooked quickly, so I went with what would be the warmest. We're having chili with peanut butter sandwiches. For dessert, we can make s'mores with roasted marshmallows, chocolate bars, and graham crackers. We have plenty of those on hand for all the kids who visit the barn."

"You know what? That sounds perfect, Hunter. You remembered—I can't eat chili without a peanut butter sandwich to go with it. And I love s'mores. I can eat them until I make myself sick."

"One patient is enough for tonight. No making yourself sick." I wink at her then turn to grab the food I made. Then I slide under the canopy and join her against the overstuffed cushions before giving her the large soup bowl by the handle.

She checks Blue again after we eat and returns with a smile. "So far, so good. He'll sleep for a while and be drunk for a while after that. When it starts wearing off, we'll know soon enough how he feels."

"I don't know what I would've done without you here, Mallory. In fact, I don't know how I've made it these last few years without you. I've missed you so damn much."

"Hunter." She says my name in a way that sounds like a mixture of a plea and a prayer.

"Hear me out, Mal. I've loved you for so long—most of my life, as a matter of fact. I've never quit loving you. Not for one single day. Not for one single minute. I need to know if you still feel the same about me."

CHAPTER THIRTEEN

Mallory

How stupid was I to think I could come home for a little more than a week and leave Cringle Cove unscathed?

I mean, just look at him, with his handsome face, mesmerizing eyes, and sexy voice. The way he looks at me with those eyes—the ones with gold flecks swimming in chocolate. They see straight through me and they always have, delving into all the secrets I thought I'd kept hidden. Like right now with his "do you or don't you love me anymore" question. I don't even know how to answer that question for myself, much less for him.

On one hand, of course, I still love him. He's been a huge part of my life for as long as I can remember. On the other hand, he crushed my heart into a million and one pieces, not leaving enough for anyone else to even attempt to put back together. Instead of a love of a lifetime, I find men with finger-like toes. Or nail fungus problems. Or they're super-clingy and ultra-creepy. All this time, I've blamed Hunter for my bad luck with men.

Tonight, I have to really look at who's to blame. Did I subconsciously pick guys who I knew wouldn't live up to my standards to avoid getting close to anyone again?

Now that I'm here with Hunter again, I'm more confused than ever. Why? Because with him, I feel better than I have in years. But I also completely resent that feeling. He makes me want to make a life with someone by my side, but not just any someone. Him. The problem is, he doesn't deserve any of that—not my love, my desire, or my future. After the way he took everything I had to give and threw it away without a second thought, he doesn't deserve absolution.

"Maybe you're right, Mallory. Maybe I don't deserve you at all. But if you still have feelings for me, even just a little, don't you think our love deserves a second chance?"

I look around me, not moving my head, but I can't seem to stop moving my eyes. They roam everywhere but toward Hunter. I can't bring myself to look at him. "Um. Did I just say all that out loud?"

"Yes, of course you did. How else could I have answered you?"

"Oh shit. That was supposed to all be in my head while I tried to sort out my thoughts and feelings before actually speaking any of it out loud. This is awkward."

"You know, I'd really like to explore how your choosing the wrong guys to date is all my fault. Except, I don't like to think about you dating any other men, so I'm all for skipping that part of it. We can focus the part about how no one else lives up to the high bar I set. If we stick to that fact and continue with that methodology, you have to agree that the only logical solution is for you to choose me."

He holds my face in his hands, the warmth of his skin heating my cold cheeks. He stares deep into my eyes, holding my gaze and silently willing me to agree with him. To give in to him. To buy into the warning sign he should be made to wear at all times.

"Mistletoe not required."

"Pardon?"

"You should have to wear that warning sign. You don't need mistletoe hanging over your head to make me want to kiss you."

"Mallory, you can kiss me anytime you want. There's no need to ask or wait for permission. All my kisses are for you anyway."

I physically hurt from how much I want that to be true…and wish it were easy to believe. Right now, I'm not ready for either.

"Hunter, I need to understand what happened before. How could you hurt me like that?" It's my turn to search his eyes for the answers to the question that has consumed me for years. The one I've been afraid to ask and afraid to hear the answer to. But to move forward, we have to go backward.

"Can't we just chalk it up to youthful stupidity and leave it in the past?" His plea sounds so earnest, I almost give in and accept that easy out.

But I know it'll just come up again later, sowing the seeds of more distrust.

"Afraid not. This is one of those need-to-know situations, and I need to know."

His resigned expression confirms he knows he has to spill the whole story, but the sadness in his eyes tells me he in no way wants to. "Okay, but you're not going to like it.

I'm not sure it'll make you feel any better about our split than you do right now."

"I'm willing to take that chance." He still doesn't know I overheard Gran that day.

"You remember my parents leased our old house, barn, and land through a property management company, right?"

"Yes. What about it?"

"At the beginning of your senior year in high school, your grandmother bought all of our land from them and became our new landlord."

My stomach drops to my knees. Why do I feel sick all of a sudden?

"A couple of months later, she cornered me and gave me an ultimatum: either break up with you, or she would evict my family from her land. That land was where my parents had built their entire business. We had so many horses and the sleighs and no options to go anywhere else with them. If my choice forced my parents to lose what they'd worked their whole lives for, I couldn't live with myself. Breaking up with you nearly killed me too, but I always thought we'd get back together somehow.

"When I heard you'd chosen to attend the University of Georgia, my whole world felt like it was imploding. I went to your grandmother's house that day and had it out with her, trying to convince her that we belonged together. She threatened my family with everything she could think of, but her hatefulness only lit a fire under me. Starting that day, I designed plans for expanding the business and making it more profitable year-round. I busted my ass day and night to get out from under her thumb."

"You bought the old horse farm outside of town." That piece of the puzzle suddenly makes sense.

"That's right. I bought that place. I bought the land across the street. Had my house built. Bought my parents their own house. I've worked harder over the last four years than I did the entire twenty-one years before that combined, and it's all paid off. Santa's Village has just as many visitors in the hottest part of the summer as it does at Christmas. Everything isn't paid off yet, but I'm well on my way."

"Santa's Village? You mean your barn up there?"

He tilts his head to the side and draws his eyebrows down. "Not just the barn, I mean all of Santa's Village."

"Wait—you own *all* of it? That place is *your* creation?"

"Yes, I thought you knew that."

"No, I had no idea." I'm nearly speechless. From everything. The threats. The fights. The way Hunter has clawed his way to the top of the town totem pole.

The prominent display of the box I gave him suddenly makes sense. Mr. Beckett won't part with it…because Mr. Beckett is Hunter.

"All I knew was I had to do something to get out from under Ernestine once and for all. After letting her rule my life once, I vowed never to give her the opportunity again."

"Why didn't you tell me? I could've stopped her." Maybe.

"That was part of her threat, of course. If I didn't tell you exactly what she said to say, or if I told you she was behind it, all bets were off. We'd be out on the curb within a week. Now that I'm older, I know it doesn't work that way, but I didn't know that at the time. I also promised myself that I'd be successful enough to prove I'm worthy of you."

"Hunter, she never thought my mom was good enough for my dad. I don't even know if she's changed her mind about that to this day. I wouldn't waste any more time worrying about what that hateful old woman thinks."

"I don't care about proving anything to her, Mallory. My promise was to prove it to you, so we'd have a chance to be together again. So you'd understand there's nothing I wouldn't do to make you happy. So you'd remember how much you used to love me. I've loved you my entire life. Nothing will ever change that. Not breaking up. Not your going off to college a thousand miles away. Not threats from Ernestine. Nothing."

Now I truly am speechless. I react in the only way that makes sense. The only response a declaration like that from Hunter could possibly elicit. With the prowess and gracefulness of a drunk gymnast, I fling myself on top of him, landing with a thud against his chest. The rush of air from his lungs sounds a lot like "oomph," but I take his arms encircling me as a positive sign.

Without another word spoken between us, I press my lips against his and inhale everything that is Hunter. His touch. His scent. My hands rest on his cheeks, lovingly holding his face when our tongues meet. His hands slide up my sides and back down again until he finds the hem of my shirt. When the warmth of his skin touches mine, my entire body ignites like an incendiary device exploded inside me.

Even though I haven't admitted how much I've missed him until now, I know it without a doubt. Every cell in my body responds only to his touch, to his caress, to his kisses. He rolls me over onto my back, removing our clothes without a fight or a hitch as he lies at my side. He uses his tongue to make love to my skin while his softly whispered words of adoration make love to my soul.

He slides over, covering me with his now naked body,

and I willingly give him free rein to do with me as he pleases. For the first time in almost four long years, we are together as one again. Tears well up in my eyes—so many tears. Tears of relief, from finally letting go of the carefree façade I've worn since losing him. Tears of happiness, from at last having the only man I've ever loved back in my arms again. Tears of love, freely given to Hunter again at last.

My first.

My last.

My only.

In the final throes of passion, it's his name that falls from my lips as my nails dig into his back. He collapses against me, his body and the heavy blankets shielding me from the wintery wind and snow. He places soft kisses on my face—lips, eyes, nose, and cheeks—kissing away my tears while his thumb languidly strokes the sensitive skin of my neck.

"Mallory Alexandra Conner, you still take my breath away."

"Hunter Alexander Beckett, I'm pretty sure that should be my line right about now."

"What happens now?" His question holds much more meaning than the simple words would normally convey.

"From the looks of things, I believe you're stuck with me for the rest of the night, Hunter. As hard as the snow is coming down and as cold as it's been, the road down the mountain will be unpassable."

"It's my very own Christmas miracle. I got the perfect present."

"What present did you want?"

"All I want for Christmas is you."

"You know that's a song, right?" I fight to keep from

smiling, but one corner of my mouth keeps lifting against my will.

"Yes, I do know that. One I wrote about you and someone blatantly stole from me. I was plagiarized and robbed blind."

"I'm certain Miss Carey would be more than willing to give you all the credit you're due."

"Nah, I can't call her again. It ended badly last time. She cried, begged me to love her. Losing me nearly destroyed her."

"How about that? I have something in common with a superstar."

"You are my superstar, Mal. And just so we're clear, maybe we were separated, but you never lost me."

"Wow. That was a great line. It actually did work for me. In fact, I think I'm ready for round two now."

"It's about damn time. I was beginning to think I'd have to make a wish for next Christmas."

WE MOVE BACK INSIDE THE BARN BEFORE FROSTBITE CLAIMS the protruding and most important parts of our bodies. We're back inside the stall, checking on Blue, when my dad calls again.

"Well, is he still good, Mallory?"

"Um, what?" I'm about to have a panic attack. Holy. Shit.

"Is Blue still doing good? How are his vitals? How's his pain management? Any new signs or symptoms I need to know about?"

"Oh, yes, Blue is still doing very well. His pain is well

managed, and he's still fairly loopy from the medication. He's not pawing, biting, or rolling on the ground."

"I'm glad to hear that because I was just checking on the roads and the weather, and it doesn't appear either of us will be going anywhere tonight. I'm sorry, sweetheart. This is the first time you've been home for Christmas in all these years, and I send you up there to get snowed in away from home."

"It's all good, Dad. Don't worry about me. The barn is warm, and there's plenty of room to sleep or even get lost in here. They have a full kitchen with food, too, and Hunter already made our Christmas Eve meal. Hopefully Blue will be much better by the time the crews plow the roads in the morning. If not, at least they'll be clear for you to come up here and see what I did wrong."

"I watched you treating him, sweetheart. You didn't do anything wrong. Blue will be just fine. It may take a few days for the colic symptoms to fully clear, but I think he's well on his way."

"How is Bear, Dad? I've been thinking about him all night. And poor Sam."

"Bear has a longer road to recovery than Blue does, but he's going to pull through. Your mom insisted on staying at the clinic tonight to keep an eye on him."

"Is Amelia back from her date yet?"

Dad chuckles to himself. "Haven't heard a word from her, Mal. Seems like she has really hit it off with Chad. Maybe she'll make it back in time for Christmas dinner tomorrow. Call me in the morning and let me know how Blue is doing."

My best friend is seeing Hunter's best friend. That would be a fun double date. Again.

"Dad, before you hang up, there's something I need to ask you."

"Okay. What's on your mind?"

"Gran."

"Hmm." His standard noncommittal response to stall the conversation for a moment while his mind whirls. "Funny how one word can encompass such a wide array of topics. What about her, specifically?"

I summarize what I overheard her saying and the whole story Hunter told me earlier to bring my dad up to speed with my racing thoughts. "How could she do that me, Dad? How could she be so cruel?"

"The best thing I know to do is to ask her directly yourself, Mallory. Look her in the eye and don't let her use any of her tactics to get out of explaining herself. She has mellowed lately and sings a very different tune for the most part. But she hurt both Hunter and you, and she should have to explain herself for that."

"You're right. She should. I'm going by her house tomorrow morning before I come home, assuming Blue is well enough for me to leave by then."

"Good idea. Stay safe up there tonight, sweetheart, and drive safely coming down the mountain. I'll see you in the morning."

"Good night, Daddy."

CHAPTER FOURTEEN

Mallory

A tickling sensation on my cheek wakes me from an incredibly realistic dream. Before I even open my eyes, I feel Hunter's warm body pressed against my back and his muscular arm draped over my waist. By the time we fell asleep, it was especially late—or very, very early, depending on how you look at it.

When I finally pry my eyes open, I find a large pair of nostrils close to my face and wiry whiskers brushing against my cheek. "Well, good morning, Blue. You seem bright-eyed and bushy-tailed this morning."

He leans into my hand when I reach up to scratch underneath his jaw. I slide off the large cot to check Blue's vitals, and Hunter turns over in his sleep, taking the blanket with him. The medication I gave Blue last night to clear his colic has already worked, and he's ready to eat again. He nudges me several times before looking at his empty feed bin. The couple of handfuls of hay I give him are gone within a few minutes, and he's looking for more, so I fill his water bucket and call Dad.

"Blue is fine now, Dad. The episode cleared, so I gave him some hay. His appetite is back full force. He ate all of what I gave him and is already demanding more. He's drinking his water, too."

"I'm glad to hear that, jelly bean. Be sure to tell Hunter to keep an eye on Blue's water intake for the next week or so to make sure he stays well hydrated."

"Okay. I'll be home soon, and we can start our family Christmas. Did Amelia make it back last night?"

"Yes, she did." Dad laughs out loud. "Chief Land brought her home on his snowmobile. She and Chad were stranded in the snow out by the lake."

"Doesn't Chad have a four-wheel-drive truck?"

"He does, but he was trying to impress her with his Mercedes sedan. It doesn't go quite as well in the deep snow."

"I'm so glad Chief Land got her instead of me this time." It's so much funnier when this happens to someone other than me.

"It's still early, jelly bean. Be careful what you say."

After I walk Blue for several minutes up and down the barn corridor, I put him back in the stall and feed him again. Hunter is still knocked out on the cot. He must've been much more tired than he showed last night. I sit down beside him and run my fingers through his hair.

"Hunter."

He rolls over and rests his head in my lap. "Why are you up so early?"

"First, it's not that early. And second, because Blue decided it was time for me to get up and feed him."

Hunter's eyes fly open, and he uses his arms to push himself up. "What? Already?"

"Yep, he's already back to normal. I've fed him, watered him, and walked him. You need to watch him over the next week and make sure he's drinking enough, but Dad thinks he'll be fine now."

"Does that mean you're leaving now?"

"I have to, Hunter. It's Christmas Day. I have to go home and spend some time with my family. But first, I'm going to Gran's house and having a talk with her. She owes me an explanation. And she'd better have a damn good one."

"Do I get to see you again later today?"

What am I doing? I'm going back to Georgia in a few days.

"You're welcome to come by whenever you're ready and hang out with us. Bring your parents if you want."

"That's a great idea. I will take you up on that and see you again very soon."

The goodbye kiss he lays on me should come with its own heat warning. CAUTION: COMBUSTIBLE.

The crews must have started early this morning because the roads have already been cleared when I leave the barn. The good news is the clear roads make it easier to get to Gran's. The bad news is the clear roads make it easier to get to Gran's.

Practicing my speech over and over makes the drive go by much faster than usual. I've got the perfect discourse all planned out in my head. Of course, the moment I see her, it'll all dissipate, and I'll blow the entire conversation within seconds.

When I pull into her driveway, I immediately notice her sitter's car isn't there, and neither is Mom's. I ring the doorbell and hear Gran's voice call out, telling me to come in. The door is unlocked, so I walk in and find her shuffling through the house with her walker to steady her gait.

"Hello, Mallory. I was wondering when you'd show up here alone to see me. Let's have a seat and put all our cards out on the table, shall we?"

"Absolutely. I think we're long overdue to face the music of the past."

She offers me a cup of coffee before taking her seat across from me. "You look like you've been out all night."

"I have been out all night—with Hunter."

"Of course you have. You never could stay away from that boy."

"He's not just a boy, Gran. He's a full-grown, successful man now. What's your excuse for not wanting us to be together?"

"I see. He told you, didn't he?"

"He did, but he didn't know that I'd actually overheard you telling him what to say when he broke up with me. Whatever lie you're planning to tell me next, don't bother. I've had your number for many years now."

"I don't have any lies left in me, Mallory. Yes, I did make him end the relationship between you two, but that was for your own good. You had the grades and test scores to go to college anywhere. But you couldn't stand the thought of leaving Hunter long enough to ensure your own future. When you started saying you didn't need a college degree and you could make enough to get by working at the grocery store ten minutes away, I knew I had to stop you from making the worst mistake of your life."

"That wasn't your decision to make."

"Maybe not, but I'd do it again tomorrow if I had to, if it helped you. Mallory, you're too smart and have too many opportunities to just throw them away. You went off to college, you got out of this small town, and you've experienced what it's like to be out on your own. Those experiences make you stronger and wiser in the long run. I'm sorry my meddling caused you pain, but you and I both know what is meant to be will be. If you're meant to be with Hunter, nothing will keep you two apart."

"Don't ever presume to interfere in my life like that again. I'm an adult, and I make my own decisions. I also make my own mistakes, and I own them. Manipulating me only makes me want to stay away from you even more than I already have. I remember how badly you treated Mom, the best woman I know, and I assure you, you will never treat me that way. I will cut you out of my life completely, and you'll never know what's happening with me."

"I've apologized to Jackie and asked her forgiveness for how I acted. I was wrong about her from the start. Pete has always loved her more than anyone, but I thought she was just after his money for the longest time."

"What money? They both went to veterinary school and have been paying off student loan debt ever since. They work hard for what they have. They sacrifice, giving up what they want to help others in need. I never understood why you called Mom a gold digger."

She sits back and stares at me in disbelief for a moment, absently circling the rim of her coffee cup with her index finger. "You really don't know, do you?"

"What do I not know? What are you talking about now?"

"Your father and you both come from a very wealthy family. My parents made a fortune on the stock market late in life. As their only child, I inherited that money when they passed. When your dad was still a baby, I started an account for him, so he'd be taken care of his entire life. I admit, I waited several years after he married your mom to finally sign the account over to him. All this time, I never knew he didn't actually use the money, though."

"He's never even mentioned it. If they didn't have the money to buy what they wanted, they waited until they saved enough."

She nods, but I think she's experiencing a deeper understanding than she's sharing with me.

"Mallory, I'm sorry for hurting you. I'm sorry for intruding into your relationship with Hunter. I'm sorry for making you not want to have a relationship with your own grandmother. I hope you'll forgive me, so I can undo all the wrongs."

"What are you not telling me?" I sense something else is going on here. The apologies. The sitters. The simple surgery that requires more medical care than usual.

"I didn't have hernia surgery. I have cancer, Mallory. I'm dying. It started a couple of years ago. I had surgery to remove the tumor before going through chemotherapy and radiation therapy. But I couldn't tolerate the treatment—it was killing me faster than the cancer was. We stopped the treatment early, knowing it would come back. And now that it has, there's nothing more they can do for me but keep me comfortable. Your mom has been spending time with me every day because I realized what a wonderful daughter she is and how lucky I am to have her in my son's life."

Tears spring to my eyes, and I feel as if the breath has been knocked out of my body by a sledgehammer to the chest.

"I-I had no idea." My words come out in a stammer from my tongue-tied disbelief.

"Now, don't be mad at your parents for not telling you. I made them promise to let me be the one to tell you. Although, I didn't want you to know before you agreed to forgive me. I'm not asking for pity—I genuinely want my granddaughter to come around. Often."

"I forgive you…and not out of pity. But because you sincerely asked me to and you apologized for what happened before. And I do want to be in your life again."

"Good. Because I'm leaving everything to you in my will. That would make it a little awkward at the reading if you still weren't speaking to me." The teasing gleam in her eye is a welcome sight. A little of the old Gran I used to know is still in there.

"To me? Why not to Daddy?"

"He refused. Your mom did too. Said they have everything they need and could ever want, and they both want you to have my estate."

"I can't tell you how unbelievably depressed that statement makes me feel. The only way that happens is if you're gone, Gran. I don't want that."

"Don't you worry about a thing, my sweet girl. Death is a natural part of life. Have you ever noticed the dates on a headstone? It shows the day you were born, and it shows the day you died, and in between, there's a dash separating them. What matters most is that you live your life to the fullest every day of that dash. I want you to remember me with happiness, not sadness. I've lived my life, and when I die, my husband will be there waiting for me on the other side. I will not be sad one bit."

We finish our coffee with Gran telling stories of when she and Grandpa were dating. Before too long, I realize she's growing tired and her skin is paler than when I arrived. She's probably been up longer than usual, just to spend time with me while I'm home.

"Gran, let's get you dressed, and you come home with me for Christmas. Spend the day with Mom, Dad, Amelia, me, and Hunter. I don't want to leave you here alone."

"I'd love that, Mallory. Thank you." Her eyes glisten with unshed tears, making mine turn on like a faucet again.

She shuffles off to her bedroom to clean up and change clothes, so I call Hunter to fill him in on her change of heart. And to warn him that she'll be at the house all day spending Christmas Day with us, just in case he changes his mind about showing up.

"I don't care who's there, Mallory. If you're there, that's all I care about. No one but you can keep me away."

"I do want you there with me, Hunter. Tell Chad to come if he wants to. He can bring his sister and niece too. Mom and Dad would be thrilled to have a house full of people today. Mom always makes too much food anyway. We'll have the huge family Christmas we've always wanted."

With Gran in tow, I rush home to shower and get dressed before all the company I've invited over shows up. As I'm jumping into the shower, I hear Gran telling Mom who all is on the way to spend the day with us. Mom squeals with delight and orders Amelia to grab more plates and silverware to set the table. When I'm fully dressed and finally presentable, I stroll back into the den and find it full of the people I love the most.

Hunter with his parents. Chad with his sister and her daughter. Amelia, Mom, Dad, and Gran round out the picture. Despite Gran's bad news about her health and the stress over the past twenty-four hours, my heart is full.

Everyone who means the world to me is right here in Cringle Cove, the very place I've avoided for way too long. The only man I've ever loved and wanted has been here all along, waiting for me to come back to my senses and back to him.

I've finally come home.

All it takes is one look at the chocolate-with-flecks-of-gold-eyed angel and I'm wrapped around his little finger.

And one day, something else golden will be wrapped around our ring fingers.

EPILOGUE

Hunter

Mallory went back to Athens four weeks ago today. Four weeks of video chats, text messages, and phone calls just isn't cutting it. I'm counting down the minutes until she graduates college. That day can't come soon enough.

The distinctive tone of the video chat ringing fills the cab of my truck. I'm waiting for her to pick up so I can see her beautiful face.

"Hello, honey. How's your day?" Her smile brightens any gloomy winter day.

"Much better now that I can see you. What are you up to?"

"I'm on a date."

"That was today?"

"Yes, it's right now, actually. I'm sitting here with my date at this very moment. Don't pretend you didn't know that when you called."

For the record, she told me about this date when she

was still home over her break. I'm not jealous that she's on a date with another guy. At all.

"Where are you? That restaurant looks very nice."

"Doesn't it? It's one of the rare four-star restaurants in this area. I can't recommend the chef highly enough, but it's really the company that makes the meal."

"In that case, I'll have——" I end the video call just as I reach her table and pull out a chair. She looks up at me with her eyes as wide open as her mouth. "I'll have whatever you're having."

"Hunter, this is Scott. Scott, this is my boyfriend, Hunter. He just surprised me by showing up here all the way from Pennsylvania."

"Hi, Scott. Nice to meet you." I extend my hand to shake his.

"Hi, Hunter." He takes my hand and gives it a firm shake. I can see why Mallory would accept a date with him. He's handsome, with blond hair and blue eyes.

"What are you doing here?" She reaches over and grabs my hand, but her eyes tell me she wishes she could do much more than that.

"My office manager said I had to use my vacation time or lose it, so I took two weeks off to come down here and spend it with you. I hope that's okay."

"You mean you were driving your mom crazy in the barn, so she threatened your life if you didn't get out of her hair for at least two weeks?"

"Semantics. You say potato, I say tomato."

"That's not the saying, Hunter."

"It is now."

With a smile in place, I turn my attention to her date. "Are you trying to steal my girl from me, Scott?"

Scott laughs, revealing his two front teeth are missing.

Another snagglepuss to add to our collection. His eyes light up with his smile, as does his face. "She's one of my teachers!"

"Hey, you're the one who took her to lunch."

"She's having lunch with the whole table. This is our school lunchroom." His eyes shine brightly with mischief.

"That's a likely story, Scott. I'll have to keep an eye on you. I can already tell." My smile shows him I'm teasing, but he already knows that.

"It's time for recess, so I gotta go now. But after recess, you have to leave because Miss Mallory promised to make me some popcorn before we watch a movie together. Just me and her."

With that, Scott jumps up from his seat, dumps his tray, and dashes outside with the rest of his class.

"You just ran off my date, Hunter."

"That's just not possible, Snagglepuss. I'm still here, and I'll always be here, just for you."

"Congratulations, Mallory. I'm so proud of you. You're officially a teacher now. This has been the longest six months of my life. Can we pack everything you own into my truck and move you back to Cringle Cove now?"

I've made more out-of-state visits over the past few months than in my entire life. But every trip has been more than worth it. Every moment with her has been better than the last. The whole time she stayed away from home, I knew I missed her—my broken heart was evidence of that. But exactly how much didn't strike me until we started spending every spare moment together—whether that was on the phone or in person.

I tried to fill the gaping hole in my life with work and money for so long. Now I know without a shadow of a doubt, only one quirky, funny, wonderful woman could possibly make me feel wealthy. The one standing in front of me, looking at me like she's completely head over heels in love with me.

She laughs as she wraps her arms around my neck. "Hunter, don't act like you haven't already loaded all my stuff into the moving truck and sent them on their way. I know you better than that."

"Fine, you caught me. I'm just trying to be efficient."

"Or, you went ahead and did it because I told you to make sure the movers were reserved over a month ago."

"Semantics. Same difference."

"Whatever you have to tell yourself to make you think you're in charge. We both know the truth, though."

"Babe, you can be in charge any time, all the time, or none of the time. Whatever you want. I only have one hard-and-fast rule that you cannot break under any circumstance."

"Oh yeah? What's that?"

"That warning label you gave me applies to us both. 'Mistletoe not required' is now our shared motto."

We seal that deal with a handshake. And by handshake, I mean a long, deep kiss that's completely inappropriate for public displays of affection. But she'll have to get used to that, because we're spending an entire lifetime together, and there will be many more kisses without mistletoe, exactly like this one.

THE CRINGLE COVE CHRISTMAS CHRONICLES

Read more about Cringle Cove in these stand-alone books:

Unexpected Gift by H.J. Bellus

What the Elf? by Kate Benson

Christmas on the Rocks by Michelle Dare

Wrapped in Love by Kristen Luciani

Winter Games by Victoria Renteria

BOOKS BY A.D. JUSTICE

Steele Security Series

Wicked Games (Book 1)

Wicked Ties (Book 2)

Wicked Nights (Book 3)

Wicked Intentions (Book 4)

Wicked Shadows (Book 5)

The Crazy Series

Crazy Maybe (Book 1)

Crazy Baby (Book 2)

Crazy Love (FREE Short Story)

Dominic Powers Series

Her Dom (Book 1)

Her Dom's Lesson (Book 2)

The Vault

Warning, Part One

Warning, Part Two

Warning, Part Three

Immortal Obsession

Immortal Envy (Book 1)

Stand-alone Romance Novels

Saving Grace

Completely Captivated

Intent

Just One Summer (Novella)

Mistletoe Not Required (Novella)

ACKNOWLEDGMENTS

First and foremost, I want to thank my Lord and Savior for His continued forgiveness of a sinner.

Readers: I'm sending an extra special THANK YOU for your support over the past few years. Releasing books is not for the faint of heart, but you make every part of this journey worth it. Every book is special to an author because it's a labor of love—every word comes from the heart. Regardless if you loved, liked, or hated the story and the characters, you still have my sincere gratitude for simply giving me a chance.

Bloggers: Thank you for your continued support. You help spread the word for cover reveals, new releases, and sales. You recommend books to your friends and followers. You are the best—for all the work you do, all the books you read, or all the promotional posts you create: THANK YOU!!!

My Editor: Lisa A. Hollett, with Silently Correcting Your Grammar, THANK YOU for always taking my books at the last possible minute with the shortest possible notice. Your side comments and our back and forth banter make the editing process a little more fun.

My Cohorts in Crime: Michelle Dare, Kate Benson, H.J. Bellus, Kristen Luciani, and Victoria Renteria, I love you ladies!!!

My Cover Designer: Dana Leah, with Designs by Dana, THANK YOU for creating the best covers that bring my characters and my story to life. What would we do without you?

ABOUT THE AUTHOR

A.D. Justice is the award-winning USA Today bestselling author of the Steele Security Series (Wicked Games, Wicked Ties, Wicked Nights, Wicked Intentions, Wicked Shadows), the Crazy Series (Crazy Maybe, Crazy Baby), the Dominic Powers series (Her Dom, Her Dom's Lesson), the Immortal Obsessions series (Immortal Envy), and a few stand-alone romance novels, such as Saving Grace, Completely Captivated, Just One Summer, and Intent.

When she's not writing, she's spending time with her own alpha male character in their North Georgia mountain home. She is also an avid reader of romance novels, a master at procrastination, a chocolate sommelier, a twister of words, and speaks fluent sarcasm. An avid animal lover, A.D. Justice has two horses, two dogs, and three cats.

While the primary focus of her books has been romantic suspense, she has expanded into different subgenres of romance. Stay tuned to read what she has in store for you!

Connect with her online!

Newsletter

Facebook Reader Group

Website

COMPLETELY CAPTIVATED

USA TODAY BESTSELLING AUTHOR
A.D. JUSTICE

SYNOPSIS

Aaron Rivers

Christa was the exact opposite of every woman who'd shared my bed for a night.

All I could think about was getting to know her intimately. She completely captivated me.

Then, as usual, I screwed up everything. My life. Her life. Our love.

Now her old crush is back in town, and he set his sights on Christa. But she's *mine*. I'll be damned if he gets her.

I will win her back before he wins her over.

Christa Lanes

Aaron breezed into my coffee shop and right into my heart. He was gorgeous, confident, and sexy.

Out of all the women who threw themselves at him, he wanted *me*.

Against my better judgment, I took a chance. Then he took our new life away.

When I was at my darkest, my lifelong friend Jared pulled me through, only to tell me he wants to take Aaron's place.

But can I give my heart to Jared when Aaron already stole it?

COMPLETELY CAPTIVATED.

PROLOGUE

The End...Or Not

July, Present Day

This is the story of two very different men who are in love with the same woman. To grasp the full impact one person has on another's life, I'm starting at what seems to be the end of the story. But don't be deceived by appearances. I'll just be getting started with my plans for them by the time you catch up with me.

Who gets the girl and lives happily ever after is yet to be seen. My part in this story will be made clear soon enough. Until then, I'd like to introduce you to Christa, Aaron, and Jared. How they started. Where they fell apart. Then you and I will see how they end up— together. This is their past. Their future is still to come.

Buckle up, buttercup. We're all going for a ride.

CHRISTA AND AARON WALKED HAND IN HAND INTO THE ultrachic, urbanely modern downtown office building. She was still reeling from their whirlwind weekend. Reality hadn't yet set in, leaving her to question if she'd hallucinated everything that had happened. A beautiful, life-changing, dream-come-true hallucination.

If I am, don't ever let me wake up, she thought.

As they crossed the marble floor of the lobby, she glanced over at Aaron for the hundredth time, convinced she was dreaming it all. A recurring unease ran through her mind and plagued her thoughts. She was desperate to ask if he felt as shocked with their new life as she did. Part of her wanted to know if the extreme mixture of excitement, fear, and exhilaration, immediately followed by sheer terror, overwhelmed him as much as it did her. But she didn't want to be *that* girl—the needy, clingy, "*What are you thinking?*" type of girl.

Her thoughts drifted to how different everything she'd ever known was compared to just a few short months ago before she'd met Aaron. Even at her young age of twenty-two, she'd learned firsthand how life wasn't fair. Her parents had made sure to teach her that valuable lesson.

She'd also accepted she'd never be lucky in anything. She'd been unlucky in having the big, loving family she'd dreamed of her entire childhood. As the only child of a deadbeat dad and a neglectful mother, the only people she could lean on were friends she'd made along the way. The Miller family had all but adopted her, giving her the only stability throughout her childhood.

Luck in money had escaped her, since she had scraped by on her very last dime for anything she'd ever had. She'd worked tirelessly to start her own business, rising early in the morning and remaining in her shop until late at night to get her café off the ground.

Finally, she'd most decidedly been unlucky in finding

love. The few men she'd made time to date turned out to be less stellar than she'd initially thought. Or dared to hope. But after the last three days, she was finally convinced her luck had changed for the better, that true love could happen, that happiness could last.

As they walked into the posh office building, nausea washed over her in repetitive waves when she realized she was completely out of place and notably underdressed. Elegant, professional women clicked by in their stiletto heels, with their hair perfectly coiffed and their nails fashionably manicured, wearing their expensive designer business clothes. Unlike everyone else, she was dressed in faded jeans, off-brand Ugg-type boots, and a generic name sweater. Her long, straight blond hair usually refused to cooperate, preferring to hang loosely on her shoulders.

She was grateful Aaron held her hand tightly in his, paying no attention to the beautiful women surrounding them. His strength flowed into her through their connected hands, giving her the courage to face whatever awaited them.

The security guard noticed her first and stood as though to stop her. The moment he realized she was with Aaron, his demeanor changed. "Good morning, Mr. Rivers."

"Good morning, Ty." Aaron dismissed the guard with a nod.

Aaron pushed the up button, and they were soon joined by several other people in the morning rush to their posh offices. Neither spoke as the elevator climbed to the twenty-sixth floor, where he led Christa to an expansive corner office.

The space was professionally decorated, with pictures and sculptures arranged to be both visually pleasing and modernly chic. The large, dark cherry wood desk was strategically placed in the corner, facing the door but not obstructing the impressive view of the city from the floor-to-ceiling windows on each side. Her back was to the door, staring out at the sights, until the angry male voice behind her caught her attention.

"Hold all my calls, Barbara." His command resembled an irritable growl when he entered the office and all but slammed the door shut behind him.

He cut his gaze to Aaron and sighed heavily without even attempting to disguise his disgust and disapproval. She watched the wordless exchange between the two men, observed as Aaron quickly averted his eyes from the heavy glare of the other man. She had a quick and powerful urge to come to Aaron's defense and put the other man in his place. The obvious question was why he'd be so disappointed in Aaron in the first place.

"Hello, I don't believe we've met before. I'm Christa." She extended her hand to offer a handshake.

"Yes, I know who you are, *Christa Lanes*. I'm Lance Rivers, Aaron's older brother." His reply was curt and brash as he blatantly ignored her proffered hand.

She immediately noticed he didn't say it was nice to meet her, and a sickening feeling about this impromptu, early morning meeting settled into her gut.

Lance's stare darted between Aaron and Christa, throwing daggers in their direction. "Have a seat." He motioned at a small conference table close to the window then jerked the chair out for himself.

Aaron took the farthest seat, putting his back to the window. Christa sat directly across from Aaron. Lance sat at the head of the small table and waited for them to settle before he began. He opened the manila folder he'd brought with him and pushed a neatly stacked collection of papers in front of Christa. He then clicked his pen and laid it directly on top of the papers.

"Ms. Lanes, let's cut to the chase, shall we? My brother, Aaron, is quite impetuous—that means he doesn't always think through his decisions as thoroughly as he should." Lance's tone was extremely condescending.

"Yes, I know what 'impetuous' means, Lance. What are you trying to say?" Christa's hackles were immediately raised, her tone rife with indignation over his assumption she was ignorant.

Lance smiled, but his eyes lacked any humor or warmth. "Everything I need to say is right there in those papers in front of you, Ms. Lanes."

Christa looked down at the papers, and her world came to a crashing halt. She couldn't breathe and couldn't form a coherent thought. The words jumped off the page at her, but in her panicked state, they were in no given order. Her mind raced and her heart throbbed, rendering her unable to comprehend the meaning of the words. Everything was a jumbled mess. But there was one lone word that resonated and reverberated throughout the echoes of her mind.

Divorce.

"I don't—I don't understand. Wh-what is this?" Christa demanded of Aaron when she finally found her voice. She searched his face intently, but it was void of any emotion. He deliberately masked his feelings, retreated inside himself, and blocked out the unpleasantness around him.

"It is exactly what it says it is." Lance spat out his sarcastic response. "Ms. Lanes, you and my brother do not have a real marriage. This fiasco never should've happened. We need to rectify this situation as soon as possible. As Aaron's lawyer, I've drawn up these papers to handle the procedures speedily."

She gripped the armrests of her chair, trying to focus on a single spot while a vortex of blackness threatened to erase her very existence. Her entire world stopped spinning and hung precariously on its axis, of that much she was sure. But the room she sat in was spinning fast enough to draw the air from her lungs, making it harder and harder for her to maintain her composure.

"Aaron. *Why?*" Desperation gripped her like a heavy vise and spilled over into her voice—forcing the pleading tone that was obvious even to her. She struggled to maintain her dignity and poise over the despair that suffused her. Everything she'd ever wanted in life was within her grasp, and she felt it slipping away, like tiny grains of sand sliding through her fingers. She was powerless to stop it.

"Ms. Lanes, surely you didn't think your relationship with Aaron was anything more than a passing fling. That's all Aaron *ever* has—just a quick fling, a one-night stand, and then he's through with them," Lance retorted, disdain dripping from his every word.

Christa heard a low growl emanate from Aaron's chest, but he didn't dispute Lance's mean-spirited words. He also didn't disagree with Lance's assessment of their relationship. She knew that was Aaron's life before her, but *they* were different. *He* was different with her. They were a couple now.

"Aaron—tell him that's not true. Tell him it's different with us," Christa pleaded.

Lance continued as if her world wasn't disintegrating all around her. Like the very person she loved the most wasn't being ripped from her life. Like her heart wasn't being cut out of her chest.

"Ms. Lanes, as you can see, Aaron is offering you a very generous settlement. You will be given ten million dollars, a house, and a vehicle of your choice, and you may keep any gifts Aaron has given you. This is the *only* time you will be offered this generous settlement." Lance's heartless words and matter-of-fact tone matched the sneer on his face.

"*What?* Ten million dollars? What are you talking about?" Unable to stay seated a second longer, Christa rose and quickly stepped around the table to sit beside Aaron. She was close enough to touch him, to feel the heat of his body, and to inhale the faint smell of his cologne. She watched him lower his head and stare down into his lap before she spoke softly to him.

"Aaron, please look at me," she requested. She watched as his Adam's apple bobbed up and down when he swallowed hard before slowly raising his chin. He turned his head toward her, his eyes indulging in a slow perusal of her body. When their gazes finally collided, she saw his emotions in the stark blue pools of his eyes before he quickly masked his feelings and his eyes became hard as nails again.

"Aaron, what's going on? Why are you doing this to us?" Christa asked softly.

She desperately wished Lance wasn't in the room so they could talk alone, and she could at least try to understand what was happening. She laid her outstretched hand on Aaron's arm and lovingly stroked his skin with her delicate fingers.

"I don't understand. I don't know why you're doing

this. But it doesn't have to be this way. We don't have to do this. We can just leave now and go home *together*."

"Let's be frank, shall we? You know who Aaron is. You and he married without a prenuptial agreement. You may have fooled him for a short time, but no judge will ever give you more than what we're offering you right now when you've only been married a few days. You are not entitled to half of everything he owns. If you want to fight us over it, rest assured we have the resources to keep you tied up in litigation for *years*, and you will not see one penny the whole time. Take the offer. Live comfortably. Move on with your life," Lance barked.

Pain and confusion were etched on her face. *I know who he is? What does he mean by that?* So many questions flew through her mind at lightning speed, too many to even try to vocalize. The only coherent thought she could latch on to was *those were divorce papers*.

Didn't we just walk in here holding hands? He brought me here to serve me with divorce papers, but I don't understand why. What's happening? The questions kept coming. They flooded her mind and made it impossible for her to make a logical decision on her own. When she sat motionless and silent for a moment too long, Lance continued.

"Ms. Lanes, it is my belief that you drugged my brother to get him to agree to marry you, and that you have continued drugging him to keep him with you for the last three days. Now that he can think clearly again, he's agreed not to press charges against you, provided you agree to this deal," Lance concluded.

"Drugged him? Press charges? I haven't done anything wrong! I don't use drugs, and I'd certainly never drug him. I wouldn't even know *where* to go to get drugs, or even *what* to get." Her gaze darted between the two brothers, waiting for one of them to speak words that made any sense to her. Her lips parted, her chest rose and fell in rapid succession, and her hands shook. Her mind was reeling, and she couldn't reconcile how Aaron could think so poorly of her.

"Aaron." The tears glistened in her eyes, spilled over her bottom lids, and poured like a torrent over her beautiful, porcelain cheeks. "You know that's not true. You know I'd never do that to you."

"Aaron doesn't remember getting married. He doesn't remember anything about the last few days with you, Ms. Lanes. These are very serious charges—you could possibly even be charged with attempted murder, if the right information was given to the police." Lance raised his eyebrows, and his tone hinted he was considering the idea of calling the police.

"You don't remember anything?" Christa barely spoke the words aloud. Lance opened his mouth to speak yet again, but she cut him off. "*Aaron*—please say something."

"No, I don't remember anything about the past three days. I don't know how we got married. How you ended up moving in with me. Nothing." Aaron's smooth, sexy voice finally found its place in the conversation.

Christa inhaled sharply, and her hand flew to her chest, covering her heart. She searched his eyes for any indication that this was some cruel, sick joke, but she found no humor in them. Nothing was there but what appeared to be contempt for her.

"You don't remember asking me to marry you, Aaron?" Christa whispered to him.

"No."

This can't be happening, she chanted silently.

"Is this what *you* want?" she asked, inclining her head toward the divorce papers.

"Yes."

She took his big hands and placed them on either side of her face, forcing him to turn in his chair to fully face her.

"When you proposed to me, you held my face like this. You said, *'Christa, you are more beautiful to me than the purest diamond. You are more precious to me than the rarest jewel. I want to be this happy every day of my life. Will you marry me?'*

"You were so loving and so sweet to me, Aaron. Even though it was already late at night, you said you were going to make Bellasara's open so we could pick out our rings and get married immediately. You said you wanted to make me yours before anyone could come along and steal me from you. I laughed because I thought you were just being funny—acting out the scenes like in the movies.

"But when we pulled up outside of Bellasara's and the door opened for us to enter, I was shocked beyond words. We searched through every bridal set before you found the exact ones you wanted me to have. Don't you remember that?"

Aaron didn't answer audibly. He only slightly shook his head to indicate *no*. He listened intently as Christa continued recanting their story through her tears. The tears that were now soaking Aaron's hands as they held her face. Her eyes, pleading with him, held his gaze steadfast, and he briefly wondered if she could read his thoughts. Without a conscious decision, Aaron's thumb lightly grazed across her face and wiped away one tear as it fell from her eyes. It was quickly replaced by another.

"You picked out my rings—the diamond engagement ring and the diamond-circled wedding band. When you found them, you told me to always remember one thing."

Christa stopped talking for a second to try to control the sob that was threatening to break free.

Aaron furrowed his brow, his eyes pinched together in the corners, silently asking her what that one thing was while he continued to watch her with rapt attention. He allowed some small amount of emotion to shine through his eyes.

Pity. He pities me. If that's what it takes to get through to him, I can endure pity for a short time.

"You said," she started and stopped to swallow a sob. "You said if I ever gave these rings back to you, it meant I was giving your love back. You said if I did that, I'd never get your love back again. You told me to hold on no matter what happened—to hold on to our love and never give it back."

Aaron's jaw muscle ticked from the hard grit he held. His breaths were quick and shallow, uncertainty and mistrust marring his handsome face. But he couldn't remove his hands from her face. Despite the terrible thoughts flying through his mind, he couldn't break the connection with her once he touched her. Everything about her had been his weakness. Her purity. Her innocence. Her admiration of him. *Had it all been a lie?* His eyes could no longer conceal the upsurge of emotion that flowed through him.

When she noticed the change in his demeanor, a seed of hope blossomed in her chest that she was getting through to him. Perhaps he did remember but suddenly had cold feet when the weekend ended and reality hit him. One thought after another swirled through Christa's mind while she tried to make sense of it all.

Did he have a change of heart?
Did he think getting married was a huge mistake?

Am I not good enough for him?

"Is this what *you* want, Aaron? You honestly don't want to be married to me? You don't want me at all?" Christa asked, leaving the tears to flow freely and her love for him to shine in her eyes.

Aaron maintained eye contact with her—gazing deeply into her eyes, looking for something, before his eyes followed the trail of her tears to where his hands cradled her face. He looked hard at the moisture gathered there. His gut told him one thing. *This was no act—no one could cry that hard, that much, and be faking her feelings. It wasn't possible.*

"I think it's best for both of us to end it now," he finally answered on a whisper.

He noted that her tears increased after his declaration, and the warm glow that shone in her eyes was slowly extinguished. He watched in slow motion as she reached up, wrapped her small fingers around his large ones, and dragged his hands off her face. The immediate emptiness slammed into him, driving deep into his core. He was losing her, losing his love, possibly even losing his destiny. *Something* vitally important was gone instantaneously, something he feared he'd never feel again.

Life had been hard for Christa, but she was no shrinking violet. She'd never felt such pain and despair. She had no doubt it would take her a lifetime to heal from the blow he'd dealt, but she didn't have it in her to roll over and give up. She reined in the minor breakdown Aaron and Lance had already witnessed, swallowed the broken heart that now resided in her throat, and straightened her spine.

"I'm not signing those papers," Christa stated with firmness but was quickly interrupted by Lance's angry growl before she could finish her sentence.

"We will see you in court in a couple of years, then!" Lance bellowed.

"I wasn't finished!" Christa yelled back before returning her gaze to Aaron, instantly softening, but maintaining her inner determination.

"As I was saying, I'm not signing those papers. Draw up a new agreement. I don't want anything from Aaron. I don't want his *money*. I don't want a *house* or a *car* or his *gifts*. I will agree to the divorce when you've taken all that out."

Looking down at her hands, she stared at the beautiful wedding rings for what felt like an eternity. She was still close enough to him that she could feel the weight of Aaron's stare on her like an iron anvil resting on her shoulders. From the corner of her eye, she knew he was also looking at her rings—the rings he chose for her. She mustered all the courage she could find as her right hand found her left ring finger. Her hands visibly trembled when she deliberately removed the beautiful diamond rings that symbolized their union.

Christa took Aaron's hand in hers, turned it over, and placed the rings in the center of his palm.

"I'm not giving your love back to you, Aaron. You're taking your love away from me. All your money, your houses, and your cars—they're all just worthless junk to me without *this*," she said as she closed his fist over "*his love,*" her wedding rings. "I won't fight you over the divorce. If you don't want me, don't love me, there's nothing to fight for." For all the boldness she tried to project, inside she only felt defeated and crushed beyond repair.

Christa rose from her chair, and Aaron's eyes followed her every movement. She wiped the remaining tears from her face and dried her hands on her jeans. Looking at

Lance, she spoke clearly. "I assume you'll contact me when you have the new papers ready for me to sign?"

Lance cleared his throat, obviously surprised by this odd turn of events. "Yes. Yes, I'll be in contact. It'll probably take about a week, though, because I have previous obligations to attend to first. I'd really prefer that we get something in writing from you today."

Christa quickly picked up the pen, drew lines through the settlement portion of the legal papers, put a big, fat zero in its place, and scribbled her initials beside it.

"Will that be good enough for now?"

Lance simply nodded, stunned, and for once in his life, speechless.

"If you honestly believe he's been drugged for the last three days, you should get him to the hospital to be tested. He may need medication to counteract any further effects." Christa's remarks were made to Lance, but she couldn't keep the true concern for Aaron out of her voice. "If he was drugged, it wasn't by my hand. I would never hurt him."

Aaron couldn't stop watching her every move. He was completely mesmerized by her, but he knew he had to break the spell. She had more natural beauty in one little pinky than all the professional models he'd *"dated"* combined. Her long, thick blond hair draped loosely over her shoulders—her shoulders that stood proud even when she wanted to break down.

Her petite frame and stature were dwarfed by his, but somehow, she had fit perfectly into his side. Her hand fit his like it was made for him and him alone. Her expressive brown eyes held nothing back, and she gave her love to him freely. Even at that moment, when she was hurt beyond measure, he had no doubt if he asked for forgiveness, she'd give it without question.

She was more honest, giving, and loving than anyone in his life, but he was pushing her away. She was the light in his dark, dreary world, and he was extinguishing her flame. He couldn't shake the feeling that she was the epitome of all that was good and pure, and he was the exact opposite. The sins of his past wouldn't let him forget what he'd done. When it came to personal relationships, his judgment had been clouded, his heart jaded. He couldn't trust his decisions or feelings, and he'd learned to bury them over the years. Regardless of the emotions she evoked, he couldn't allow himself to give in.

Christa wiped her face again, reeled in her emotions, and stepped toward the door. She was only a few feet away from Aaron, but it may as well have been miles. Christa was simply trying to keep her composure until she could get back to her small apartment and have a total breakdown in private. She didn't want the workers in the pretentious office to see the telltale signs of her ugly crying—red-rimmed, puffy, blood-shot eyes, red nose, and tear-streaked cheeks. Her sole focus now was to get to the elevators as quickly as possible, but Lance's next comment stopped her dead in her tracks.

"Ms. Lanes, there's one more delicate subject we need to discuss before you leave." Lance was almost hesitant, and he nervously cleared his throat. Christa knew whatever was coming next couldn't be good.

"And what's that? What more could you possibly want from me?" she asked incredulously as she whirled around to fully face him.

Lance cleared his throat again, something she noticed he did when he wasn't comfortable. "I need you to list anyone with whom you've ever had sexual relations. In the event you try to claim that you're pregnant before this divorce is final, I assure you we will require a vast measure of tests to be performed to confirm paternity."

Lance knew demanding that information was a far stretch if it came down to a fight in a court of law. She didn't have legal representation present, and they didn't have a prenuptial agreement. He knew he didn't have a valid reason for requesting this information at this point, but he was banking on the fact that she had no legal knowledge or training.

She didn't know the wicked ways in which he could use this information against her if she later changed her mind and pursued the path to gain a full half of Aaron's considerable assets. But he needed to make sure his brother and their fortune were safe and secure from any gold-digging harlots.

Lance pushed a blank sheet of paper across the table in her direction. She looked from Lance to Aaron, clearly unsure of what she should do, and silently praying that Aaron would come to her rescue. But he sat stone silent, patiently waiting for her to complete the embarrassing and humiliating task Lance had asked of her.

Christa stepped to the table and scribbled a couple of words before shoving the paper back at Lance. He balked when he read the paper. "Ms. Lanes, I need you to list *everyone.*"

"I did," she responded indignantly, then turned her head to look Aaron squarely in the eye.

Unable to contain his curiosity of what the paper held any longer, Aaron grabbed the paper from Lance's grip. He couldn't believe his eyes. He looked from the paper to

Christa's face, closely examining her while he tried to come to terms with what he saw.

"It only has my name on this paper," Aaron stuttered disbelievingly.

"I know. I was waiting for the right man. I told you that on our wedding night," she said as the blush crept up her face. If Aaron had to guess, he would say she was clearly remembering their first night together. The night he couldn't remember at all. He suddenly wished he could remember that night more than any other night he'd ever spent in a woman's arms.

Aaron stared back down at his name on the paper. The shame and guilt immediately started building in his chest. He knew people—he could read them like a book. He knew in his gut that she was telling the truth. She was still so young at twenty-two, mostly isolated and completely introverted, and didn't engage with anyone outside her small circle before he came along and charmed her. She'd been a virgin until he took that away from her. On top of ruining her life, he was divorcing her after not even remembering marrying her.

Aren't I quite the catch? he thought to himself. *She'll be better off without me.*

When he finally looked up, he noticed the door to Lance's office was standing wide open, and Christa was gone. Her rings were still in one of his clutched fists, and the paper that contained only his name was in the other.

And Aaron was completely alone.

TABLE FOR TWO

April

"Christa, the delivery man is here. Can you watch the front while I handle our delivery?" Allie asked.

"Sure, Allie. I got it," Christa responded.

Allie Barker was Christa's best friend and only employee at her coffee shop and bakery, The Sweet Spot, but somehow, they made it work together day after day. When the small shop in the high-rent district of an influential San Francisco neighborhood became available at an amazingly affordable price, Christa took it as a sign that it was meant for her. The fact that it had a ready-to-use gourmet chef kitchen was an additional bonus.

She thought if she could get her business going with fast and easy treats first, the kitchen would be perfect for catering larger events later. She had a five-year plan and was determined to see every last detail through to fruition. She was so involved in her thoughts about those plans, and how her business was performing, she didn't hear the bell over the door chime when the next customers walked in.

When she looked up, she was pulled into the deepest, most delicious sea of blue ever to grace a man's face. He was more than handsome—he was drop-dead gorgeous. His blue eyes sparkled with mischief, his smile was warm and contagious. She felt her own cheeks lifting in response.

His dark black hair was naturally messy and sexy, perfect for the obligatory finger-gripping during wild, swinging-from-the-rafters sex. His face was covered in just the right amount of five-o'clock shadow. He was tall, with broad shoulders, a narrow waist, and had a finely sculpted chest, if the shirt stretched tight across his shoulders was any indication. He had just the right amount of muscular build to be athletic.

Unfortunately, he'd walked in with an equally beautiful woman by his side.

As if I had a chance with him anyway, Christa thought to herself.

She pasted her best hostess smile on her face and greeted her new customers, mentally reminding herself she needed the clientele more than she needed a date.

"Hello. Welcome to The Sweet Spot. What can I get you?" she asked cheerfully.

"Hello." The sexy, baritone voice was like smooth velvet to her ears. "Can we get a large regular coffee and a medium skinny white chocolate mocha, please?"

"Sure. Just have a seat, and I'll bring it out to you. Anything from the pastry case?" Christa offered, practicing her salesperson skills.

The tall stick figure that accompanied the Adonis standing before her replied with disdain dripping from her lips. "Oh, those things have a million carbs. Keep them away from me."

As if on cue, the handsome man responded with the opposite. "They look delicious. How about one of those croissants—toasted, with plenty of butter on the side?"

Christa wasn't certain, but she would've sworn he ordered the pastry just to antagonize his date. She rang up the sale, quickly filled the coffee cups, and delivered the order to their table.

"Aaron, really, did you have to get the croissant? It's the biggest pastry in the case," the stick figure whined.

Aaron picked up the pastry and sank his teeth in. "Oh my God!"

Christa had turned her back to him the second before she heard his exclamation. She whirled around, placed her hand on his shoulder, and leaned in close to him. "What's wrong?"

He almost laughed at the concern on her face. "Absolutely nothing is wrong. This is *the best* croissant I've ever had. Where do you buy these?"

He watched her beautiful face turn the loveliest shade of pink as her embarrassment set in. She quickly snatched her hand from his shoulder and straightened her back. "Umm, I don't buy them. I make them here."

"I'm impressed—honestly. This is heaven. It literally melts in my mouth."

"I'm glad to hear that." Her reply was as warm and honest as her returned smile.

"I'll have to come here every day now," he said with a playful wink and a knowing smile. A smile that said he knew affected her and he knew she wished she could hide her reaction from him.

He'd always had the same effect on the ladies, and he'd frequently used his good looks to his advantage. He'd learned to read the signs; he knew when they were interested in him, and what they wanted from him. He'd give them a good time for a night or so, but no one ever held his interest for too long.

As he watched her walk away, he contemplated how he wouldn't mind that little lady being next on his list. He was well-known in the influential celebrity and business circuits and often dated high-profile models. *Dated* was a generous term. He wined, dined, and sixty-nined them, then sent them on their way. His work had him hip-deep in models on a daily basis. Models that were long-legged, skinny, and wouldn't eat more than a couple of pieces of dry lettuce to avoid gaining an ounce.

But everything about her seemed to contradict his normal type. Her name tag read *Christa*. She couldn't have been over five foot three barefoot. She didn't have long legs like his current companion, the one whose name he'd already forgotten. Christa had curves in all the right places, like a real woman should. Her breasts were small but perky, her legs were short but sleek and muscular, and her perfectly round ass—he could feast on it all day.

Her hair was long and blond, but it was her amazing brown eyes that held the magic. They captivated him, reached out and physically touched him, holding him as her hostage. For the first time in his adult life, he decided he'd gladly give full control over to someone else. The term *love at first sight* had always been a cliché to him. He'd argued there was no way a person could fall in love when they first met. But the feeling that stirred in his chest told him this pure, natural beauty was a threat to his one-night-only rule.

He watched her as she returned to the counter, took a few orders, and gave every customer her personal touch as she filled their orders. He was amazed at how she made each person feel like a welcome guest in her home, and they were all glad to be there. His eyes followed as she continued to move around the room, talking to her patrons as if they were long-lost friends. She adjusted pastries in the case and refilled the carafe with hot coffee with ease and care.

She returned to his table a few minutes later. "Can I warm you up?"

His lips curled into a slow, sensual smile. He intentionally misinterpreted her offer and his playful eyes danced with mischief. "I wasn't aware that was a menu choice."

When she realized her choice of words, he watched with amusement as the red crept up her neck and face.

"Your *coffee*," she clarified with a laugh, thankful that his date was on the phone and completely oblivious to their conversation.

"I'm good," he responded, lifting one eyebrow and deliberately leaving his response open to interpretation. Christa's face suddenly looked like she had a sunburn, and he was completely enamored with her. "Keep blushing like that, and I might start to think you like me."

She laughed nervously and straightened imaginary wrinkles from her clothes. "We can't have you thinking that, can we?"

The next day, Aaron showed up with a different girl—same build, same attitude, but his attention was transfixed on Christa. They continued their playful banter, with Aaron making comments to ensure Christa knew he was more than interested in her. Her natural shyness around men was evident, but that was part of his intense attraction to her and the foremost reason why he tamed his approach. She wasn't seeking attention, fame, or fortune. She was genuinely a beautiful person, inside and out, and he wanted to get to know her and see where their mutual attraction took them.

"Hi, Christa. Did you save any of your delicious, mouthwatering croissants for me?" Aaron asked in his smooth as silk, sexy bedroom voice as he strolled up to the counter.

Christa smiled through her awkwardness. "I might have one or two left."

"Feel free to save me one every day. I'll have to add some extra time to my work-out schedule to make up for it, but it's so worth it," he joked, patting his already muscular stomach.

Over the following week, Aaron came in alone and ordered his usual. Their witty dialogue increased daily along with their comfort level. When he couldn't wait any longer, he decided to make his move when Christa delivered his order to his table. He put on his best smile and held out his hand. "I haven't introduced myself. I'm Aaron Rivers."

"Christa Lanes," she replied as she accepted his hand.

"I'd really like to have breakfast with you, Christa."

Confusion shrouded her face. "Umm, right now?"

He nodded, his genuine smile covering his face, and gestured to the empty chair. "Right now would be perfect."

Christa looked around her café and decided Allie had everything under control. "One minute." She scurried behind the counter and grabbed her cup of coffee and a caramel croissant, a brand-new menu item she had just perfected the night before. She hurried back to his table and slid into the chair across from him.

His eyes bugged out at the sight of Christa's pastry. She giggled as he looked back and forth at their plates, trying to figure out the difference between the flaky pastries.

"What is *that*?" he asked spiritedly, while never taking his eyes off the deliciousness on her plate.

"It's something new I'm trying out to see how customers like it. It's a caramel croissant. My own concoction." She finished speaking as she raised her fork to cut off a bite. Before the tines touched her pastry, Aaron snatched her plate away and replaced it with his own.

"Let me be your guinea pig." He vigorously dove into the baked bliss, licking his lips while never taking his eyes off it. Christa watched his facial expressions for his reaction, her teeth leaving their imprint on her bottom lip in anticipation. She didn't have to wait long to know exactly what he thought about it.

"Fuck. This is incredible, Christa. This is the best thing I've ever eaten. It almost tastes better than sex feels." Then, as if it suddenly hit him, his expression turned serious as he continued. "I can't believe you gave me the plain one and took the caramel one for yourself."

She laughed heartily as she explained her duplicity. "Honestly, I had a feeling you'd take this one away from me as soon as I brought it out. It actually took you a little longer than I thought it would. I almost got a bite of it. You were a little slow on the uptake. Maybe I gave you too much credit, after all."

They settled into a playful banter, enjoying the company throughout the rest of their breakfast. With the pair feeling at ease with each other, their conversation moved easily from one topic to another, questions and answers freely shared as they became better acquainted.

When the coffee and croissants were finished, Aaron reluctantly rose from the table.

"I have to get to work now. Can we do this again tomorrow morning?"

Christa was in awe of his confidence. He was so sure of himself, and he had no fear of rejection. *Then again*, she thought, *why would he?* He was beautiful, and she was... well, she didn't feel like she was in his league. But he made it a point to come into her establishment, ask to have breakfast with her, and he wanted to do it again. Those had to be positive signs.

Christa rose from the table and smiled as she nodded. "I'd like that."

She watched him leave while she picked up their plates and began preparing for the lunch crowd. Allie slid up beside her, smiling broadly while she watched Christa watching Aaron.

"You like him."

"He's funny. But I'm definitely not his type." Christa sighed to herself, refusing to get caught up in the "I wish" world she could easily lose herself in. She'd wished her childhood away. That sentiment had gotten her nowhere. Her new focus was "I will," and she only focused on the goals she knew she could attain.

Aaron Rivers wasn't one of those attainable goals.

"He may be funny, but he's not the only one. You're funny if you think I can't see through you, Christa Lanes. You definitely like him, and he seems to be into you too. Now, if you'd just let him *get into* you...if you know what I mean."

Christa lowered her head and covered her forehead with her hand. She shook her head and chuckled at her best friend. "Did you defrost the meat for lunch like I asked you to?"

"You know, C, you should've asked that hunk about lunch meat before he left."

"This is why I can't have anything nice."